BEYOND THE GATHERING STORM

Books by Janette Oke

Another Homecoming* / Tomorrow's Dream*
Beyond the Gathering Storm
Celebrating the Inner Beauty of Woman
The Father of Love
Janette Oke's Reflections on the Christmas Story
The Matchmakers
The Meeting Place* / The Sacred Shore*
Nana's Gift
The Red Geranium
Return to Harmony*

CANADIAN WEST
When Calls the Heart   *When Breaks the Dawn*
When Comes the Spring   *When Hope Springs New*

LOVE COMES SOFTLY
Love Comes Softly   *Love's Unending Legacy*
Love's Enduring Promise   *Love's Unfolding Dream*
Love's Long Journey   *Love Takes Wing*
Love's Abiding Joy   *Love Finds a Home*

A PRAIRIE LEGACY
The Tender Years   *A Quiet Strength*
A Searching Heart   *Like Gold Refined*

SEASONS OF THE HEART
Once Upon a Summer   *Winter Is Not Forever*
The Winds of Autumn   *Spring's Gentle Promise*

WOMEN OF THE WEST
The Calling of Emily Evans   *A Bride for Donnigan*
Julia's Last Hope   *Heart of the Wilderness*
Roses for Mama   *Too Long a Stranger*
A Woman Named Damaris   *The Bluebird and the Sparrow*
They Called Her Mrs. Doc   *A Gown of Spanish Lace*
The Measure of a Heart   *Drums of Change*

———

Janette Oke: A Heart for the Prairie
Biography of Janette Oke by Laurel Oke Logan

*with T. Davis Bunn   00C

JANETTE OKE

BEYOND THE GATHERING STORM

BETHANY HOUSE PUBLISHERS
MINNEAPOLIS, MINNESOTA 55438

Published by Bethany House Publishers
A Ministry of Bethany Fellowship International
11400 Hampshire Avenue South
Minneapolis, Minnesota 55438
www.bethanyhouse.com

Printed in the United States of America by
Bethany Press International, Minneapolis, Minnesota 55438

ISBN 0–7642–2400–X (Trade Paper)
ISBN 0–7642–2401–8 (Hardcover)
ISBN 0–7642–2403–4 (Large Print)
ISBN 0–7642–2402–6 (Audio)

The Library of Congress has catalogued the regular edition of this book as follows:
Library of Congress Cataloging-in-Publication Data

Oke, Janette, 1935–
    Beyond the Gathering Storm / by Janette Oke.
        p. cm.
    ISBN 0–7642–2401–8 — ISBN 0–7642–2400–X (pbk.)
    1. Royal Canadian Mounted Police—Fiction. 2. Brothers and sisters—Fiction. 3. Edmonton (Alta.)—Fiction. 4. Police—Canada—Fiction.
I. Title.
    PR9199.3.O38   B49   2000
    813'.54—dc21   00–009397

this book beLong's to
Gourtnye Gossman

JANETTE OKE was born in Champion, Alberta, during the depression years, to a Canadian prairie farmer and his wife. She is a graduate of Mountain View Bible College in Didsbury, Alberta, where she met her husband, Edward. They were married in May of 1957 and went on to pastor churches in Indiana as well as Calgary and Edmonton, Canada.

The Okes have three sons and one daughter and are enjoying the addition of grandchildren to the family. Edward and Janette have both been active in their local church, serving in various capacities as Sunday school teachers and board members. They make their home near Calgary, Alberta.

CHAPTER 1

The cold rain and wind did not make for the kind of morning she would have chosen for the day's venture. Though she did her best to shield herself with the borrowed umbrella, it was impossible to keep either wind or rain from penetrating her clothing. It wasn't the weather itself she found hard to endure. The fact that distressed her was her father's having just spent three days with her as she carefully chose a new, though limited, wardrobe. Was it to be ruined on her first day and all that time wasted? Her father had not complained, but she was sure he thought the decision making could have been compressed just a bit.

She had been nervous enough when leaving her small room in the boardinghouse, and the weather did not help. "I wish Dad could have stayed—or Mama could have come with me," she whispered to herself.

She remembered her mother's parting reassurances, even though the tears streaming down that familiar face had seemed to belie them. *"God will be with you. Never forget that. And we'll be praying. Every day,"* her mother had whispered.

That thought had a steadying effect, and she clutched the umbrella more tightly and prepared to cross the street.

She had lifted a foot to step out when she heard an approaching auto. Automatically her head turned and she paused, still amazed and amused by the noise and the speed with which these modern conveyances traveled. This one was dark blue with a fancy piece of statuette embellishing the hood. The man at the wheel was poking his head out the open window, obviously for better vision than through the rain-spattered windscreen. Dark goggles covered his eyes and a long scarf dangled from his neck, threatening to whip away in the wind.

She could not help but stare, a bemused smile lifting the corners of her mouth. Momentarily she forgot the rain and her nervousness, so taken was she with the car speeding along the sloppy, rain-drenched street.

She shifted her umbrella so it would not block her view and stepped to the edge of the sidewalk.

Too late she recognized her mistake. A spray of dirty rainwater splashed over her skirts as the automobile shot by. She scrambled back in alarm, but the damage had already been done. She looked from her dripping garment to the departing auto. The driver thrust his head out the window again to cast a backward glance her way. Maybe he was going to pull over and rush back to apologize. He merely shrugged his shoulders in an exaggerated fashion, then had the nerve to grin and wave. She could not believe his rudeness. This would never happen back home. She was sure her new clothes were ruined, and this man seemed to think the whole thing was some harmless lark.

"Oh dear," she exclaimed as she looked in dismay at her wet skirt. She was to have a job interview—in the building just across the street. Her father had arranged it, had hoped to accompany her, but duty had called and he'd had to leave the city. Now here she was, her clothing a mess, her shoes soaked, and no time to go back to change.

"What do I do now?" she asked aloud, her eyes wide with consternation. "I can't—" She shook her head, then started to laugh. "Well—I'll have to. There's nothing else to be done. I guess I'll just have to make the best of it."

She studied the street carefully to make sure there were no more approaching automobiles, then darted across, the umbrella trailing along over her shoulder. She was already such a mess that a little more rain was not going to make much difference.

She pushed through the heavy lobby door and stood disconsolately gazing around. No one seemed to be in sight, and she wasn't quite sure which of the doors leading off this wide entry was the one she should be taking. She closed the umbrella, placed it in the stand, and tried vainly to shake the water from her skirts. "Mama always said that life can bring some nasty surprises and one has to learn to just make do," she whispered to herself as she smoothed her dark hair back under her hat. "Well, I'm not quite sure how to 'make do' this time."

She brushed at her coat the best she could, noting that it had taken the worst of the muddy splash, though her new gray skirt also had a dark streak across the front panel.

She removed the coat. She could turn the worst where it would not be seen. With a fresh hankie she wiped the raindrops from her face and again patted self-consciously at her damp hair. She straightened her shoulders and took a deep breath, willing the assurance of her mother's prayers. Then she cast another quick look around.

She had taken only a few steps when she thought of the umbrella. It was borrowed. What if someone thought that the umbrellas in the stand were for public use? And maybe they were. She had no idea about city ways. She turned and retrieved it from the stand, though it was difficult to carry both the dripping umbrella and her damp coat.

Dad said, "Up the stairs and to the right," she reminded herself. *The man's name is Kingsley. Arthur Kingsley—but I need only remember Mr. Kingsley—sir.* She forced another smile and squared her shoulders. It was indeed an adventure—just as her father had said. She cast a rueful look downward and determinedly climbed the last step and turned to her right.

Dad said there is a receptionist. I am to

speak with her. Introduce myself and tell her my business.

She grimaced and moved the coat in an attempt to cover the front of her skirt. What would the lady think about her appearance?

"I do hope she has a sense of humor," she muttered.

She found the room at the end of the hall and hesitated only a moment before entering at the sign's invitation. *Arthur Kingsley and Associates. Please come in.*

There were a number of people in the room. Desks lined one full wall, and at least a half dozen women were bent over typewriters as fingers beat out rhythms on the black-and-white keys. In a row of chairs near the door, other individuals waited, shifting impatient feet this way, then that, seemingly intent on catching the nearby receptionist presiding at the desk. The papers stacked about her nearly obscured the sign that read *Miss Stout, Receptionist.* The young girl breathed a relieved sigh, then could not hide another smile as she moved toward her. The middle-aged woman who bore the name of Miss Stout was as thin as a cattail reed.

"Yes?" said the woman without even glancing up from her papers.

The solitary word caused all heads in the room to lift and concentrate on the lone figure near the desk. The girl felt a moment of panic, then cleared her throat, managed a weak smile, and spoke with more confidence than she felt. "I am Christine Delaney. I have—" For a brief moment the word escaped her. Mentally she scrambled to save herself a great deal of further embarrassment. "I have an appointment with Mr.—ah—Mr.—" Another moment of panic while she tried to think of the name. "Mr. Kingsley. Mr. Arthur Kingsley" suddenly burst from her, and she drew in a relieved breath.

The woman frowned.

"But I do have a bit of a problem," Christine hurried on, surprised at her boldness. "Just as I was crossing the street here"—she waved her hand in the general direction of the offending street—"this car swished by and splashed my skirt. Maybe Mr. Kingsley would prefer that I make another appointment—for later—when I look more presentable. . . ."

Christine faltered to a stop as the woman's frown deepened.

"Crazy drivers," Miss Stout finally spat out. "They should have never been allowed on the streets. They don't care how they drive."

"Oh, I—"

"I've had to jump out of their way two mornings in a row," the woman continued, by now thoroughly worked up. "And it's not just the puddles. You take your life in your hands. They never should have allowed them. Never. Autos and people just don't belong on the same streets—that's what."

All the time she was talking, the woman was stacking and shifting papers with such vengeance that her desk fairly shook. Christine heard a tittering from one of the desks to her left. The woman must have heard it, too, for she sent a dark scowl in that direction. Typewriter keyboards began to clack with renewed energy.

"Come," said the woman, nodding her head toward Christine as she rose from the desk.

"But shouldn't I—?" she began, glancing down once more at her skirt.

"Mr. Kingsley is a very busy man. He doesn't have time to set up another interview. He wants the matter settled—today. You'll just have to make the best of it."

Make the best of it. Hadn't she heard those words all of her life? Christine

16

shrugged and turned to follow.

"And leave your coat and that umbrella over there. We won't have them dripping on the carpet," said the woman curtly, her frown expressing her attitude toward both items as she pointed to the coat-tree across the room.

Christine obediently hung her new coat beside four others, hoping it and her borrowed umbrella would be safe. She meekly followed the rather impatient woman through the massive oak door, glad to be out of sight of the curious eyes.

The room was a large one, filled with shelves and tables and file cabinets, all overflowing with papers and bundles and stacks of ledgers. In the middle of the room a large man occupied a big desk and chair. His head was bent forward, and straying strands of salt-and-pepper hair made him look like some strange creature with a shaggy mane. Oversized hands were busy tracing a line on the pages spread out before him. Christine could hear mutterings that included unfamiliar words and expressions she was sure her mother would never have allowed in her house. Judging from the tone and the dark scowl that creased his face, it appeared that

Mr. Kingsley was displeased about something.

"Sir," the receptionist began in a deferential manner.

The only reply was a growl of acknowledgment.

"Your last interview is here, sir."

He did not raise his head. "I hope she's better than the others," he groused. "Can't type. Can't spell. I don't know what they teach them in schools these days. I'd be spending my whole time—"

"Sir. I have her with me."

The head came up. Two deep brown eyes peered out at Christine from beneath bushy brows. An even deeper frown made rutted folds from one side of his forehead to the other. Two large hands reached up to push the abundance of wild hair back from his face.

He did not speak. Nor did Miss Stout. Christine swallowed in discomfort—but she did not move. Who should break this awkward silence? Dared she?

She did.

"I am Christine Delaney," she said in a surprisingly even voice. "I have an appointment—an interview—for a job. I must apologize. I . . . I had a little mishap on the way here. This auto—"

"Fool drivers," sputtered the man in echo of the receptionist's sentiments. His gaze fell to her skirt as her hand gestured helplessly. "Have no respect for anyone on the sidewalks. You would think the streets were invented just for them to run their fool machines. Drive like Jehu. The whole lot of 'em. Don't know what's worse—the dust or the mud."

He shifted his gaze back to Christine's face. "So I suppose you need to rush home to change?" he queried, irritation in his voice.

"No, sir," she responded quickly, a hint of amusement touching her respectful tone. "That is—if *you* don't mind, sir."

He looked surprised at her reply and leaned further to take another look at her. "Your shoes are wet," he noted gruffly. "You'll catch your death of cold."

Christine merely shrugged. "If wet shoes were likely to kill one," she said lightly, "I would have been gone long ago."

This seemed to surprise him even more. He cleared his throat. Christine noticed the frown lines were not as deep. "Well, let's get on with it then," he said, his voice almost civil.

Christine heard the door close softly. Miss Stout had withdrawn.

He reached for a file the receptionist had left on the corner of his desk.

"Any previous work experience?" he quizzed before his eyes even scanned the contents.

"No, sir. At least not in typing," responded Christine.

He lifted the shaggy brows. "What in?"

"Whatever my father or mother saw fit to assign," she answered truthfully.

He looked amused at that. "So you're telling me you can follow orders?"

"Yes, sir. I believe I can."

"And you're not afraid of work?"

She did not hesitate. "We were expected to do our share," she replied. "Work was part of life. Survival depended upon it."

He nodded.

"Well, that's better than most these days," he said grudgingly and gave his immediate attention to the file in his hands.

"Oh yeah," he said after a moment, his head coming up. "You're that Mountie's kid. Spent your whole life up north." His eyes turned back to her. "Bet this is some different, eh?"

Christine could not avoid a quick glance at her skirt. To her surprise, she heard him chuckle.

"Well, one thing you'll learn fast enough is to watch out for those fool drivers. You take your life in your hands every time you walk the street. Should never have allowed autos in the first place. Now the whole city is overrun with 'em. Never get 'em off the street now. It's gotten so you have to own one—just to hold your own against the rest of 'em."

Christine smiled. She did hope he would soon get down to the interview. Her wet feet were uncomfortable, and she was still experiencing a case of nerves over searching for her first real job. What if she didn't get it? What was she to do next? Her father had planned to stay on until she was well settled. Now she was alone. Alone and nervous. And totally out of her element.

He closed the file. She felt her heart sink. He had not given her a fair chance. Had barely read anything written there.

"Hand this to Miss Stout on your way out," he said briskly. "You start Monday morning. Eight o'clock—sharp. She'll fill you in on the details."

Christine had the job. She had the job, and she had not even been interviewed. At least not as secretary school had led her to believe. She accepted the closed file woodenly, managed a mumbled "Thank you, sir," and turned to go, still in shock.

"And, Miss Delaney," he called after her when she was almost to the door.

She turned. So she had indeed misunderstood. Now the truth would come out.

"You best get on home as fast as you can and change those shoes—just in case," he said, almost kindly. "Wouldn't want you coming down with a cold, now, would we? Before you even start your first job."

She smiled and nodded in agreement.

She had just shrugged into her coat and safely gathered up the umbrella when there was a bustle of activity at the door. She did not at first see who entered, but she did notice the arrival caused a great deal of stir in the room.

Christine saw that Miss Stout's sour expression became even more grim as her lips pursed in disapproval. But in the row of desks forming the secretary pool, the response was much different. Heads came up and hands reached to tidy hair. Coy glances and soft fluttering of eyelashes accompanied knowing smiles. Christine turned to see who had brought such a startling response. And there he stood, dripping goggles dangling from a gloved hand, the long scarf carelessly flung about his neck and across one shoulder, an arrogant lift to his head as his eyes surveyed the row of young typists. He was unmistakably the driver of the auto who had splashed her so thoroughly and dismissed it with a careless shrug and a mocking grin.

She felt her back stiffen, her lips compress.

He swung around to look at her and their eyes met. She could tell he recognized her immediately. His glance fell to her splattered coat.

"Looks like you were standing too close to the curb," he joked. His dark eyes crinkled in amusement.

"Apparently," she responded stiffly, her voice cool and even. "Miss Stout and Mr. Kingsley have both assured me that I will soon know better. They say the city is filled with drivers who care little about others."

One dark eyebrow rose. He obviously

23

was neither repentant nor apologetic. In fact, he still looked amused. But his next words surprised her. "Just give me a minute and I'll give you a ride home."

His tone seemed to imply that he was bestowing a great favor. Christine could sense the whole room go still.

"No, thank you," she said without hesitation. "It might be dangerous walking through the streets, but I prefer to take my chances."

Without looking at him again, she gathered the materials Miss Stout had given her to read over the weekend and turned to the door. Everyone in the room seemed to have their eyes on her. She didn't care. She hoped they did not think she knew this arrogant young stranger.

She was just about to open the door when she heard him say, "Is Father in?"

"This is a workday," Miss Stout answered crisply. "Where else would he be?"

"Good" came the terse reply.

"He's busy right now . . ." the woman began as Christine's head swiveled around in shock.

"He's always busy." The young man totally ignored the outstretched hand of the receptionist. Without a moment of hesitation, he flung open the door to Mr. Kingsley's office.

Christine's heart nearly stopped as she realized she had just exchanged unpleasantries with the boss's son. Before she could even catch her breath, she heard Mr. Kingsley's loud voice. "There you are. And just in time. Give that young woman out there a ride home. Some idiot driver nearly drowned her in road muck."

CHAPTER 2

"Is something troubling you?"

Henry Delaney's head swiveled toward the questioner, and his mouth opened to make quick denial. But as his dark eyes met the intense blue of those of the man who sat before the open fire, he closed his mouth without a word being uttered. He stopped his agitated pacing and brushed at the trim mustache covering his upper lip. It was the only habit he had never conquered in his effort to give nothing away.

His father no doubt picked up on it now when he said, "Is it something to do with the Force?"

The younger man heaved a deep sigh. How could he answer that? It wasn't—yet in a way it was. He ran one finger over the length of the lip again and turned back to the fire. The husky at his father's feet stirred restlessly, looking from one to the other as though waiting for some kind of exchange to take place.

"Sometimes I hate the Force," Henry muttered and then stiffened, his face flushing guiltily as if he had just committed treason.

The older man did not respond. Just nodded toward the chair opposite him before the open fire. The dog lifted his head, a soft whine coming from somewhere deep in his throat.

With a heavy sigh, the young man lowered himself to the seat.

"I'm sorry," he began slowly. "I didn't mean to bring my . . . my discontent with me. I have looked forward to this little break for so many months. I . . . I have no wish to spoil it for—look, can we just sort of keep things, you know, between us? Mother has been looking forward to having this Christmas together. I don't want her hearing about my problems."

The older man smiled. "Your mother asked me to speak with you."

Henry's face showed his alarm. Then he reached up to tug on his mustache again. "It was that obvious?"

"I thought you hid it very well. Almost had me fooled. I assumed that you might just be tired. One gets that way after months of duty. But your mother—she's not so easily fooled."

The young man leaned forward, his elbows on his knees. Now that it was out in the open, he felt relieved.

"It's not the Force, Dad. I still . . . still love being part of the RCMP. I can't imagine being anything else." He ran a hand through thick brown hair. "It's just—well, some of the tasks we are called upon to do. It's almost a mockery of our motto. 'To protect and to serve.' That's a pretty tall order. To serve isn't so difficult. But how does one—can one—protect, in complex circumstances far beyond our control?"

Wynn Delaney stirred. "I think your mother will be relieved. She thought—we both feared it might be rumors of war that had you concerned."

Henry turned in surprise. "You really think we'll be involved?"

Again Wynn shifted in his seat, his eyes turning to the flames in the fireplace as though seeking an answer in the blaze. "I'd like to think not, but things are looking worse all the time."

He looked toward his son. "Have you been able to keep up with news of what's going on with Hitler in Europe?"

Henry shook his head. "Only smatterings—now and then—and I never know how accurate those bits and pieces are."

"Sometimes I wonder about their accuracy myself. But it is looking more and more like they might need our help over there."

"And Mother thinks I may consider going?"

Wynn nodded.

There was silence for many minutes before Henry spoke again. "I don't know . . . at this point. If—and when—it happens, I'll have to do some praying about it. I admit it would be hard to stay if I felt my country needed me over there. I'll be praying," he said again.

Wynn's eyes stayed focused on his son. Henry was pretty sure his dad was thinking about how many other Canadian fathers and mothers were facing the heart-wrenching possibility of watching sons—and daughters—march off to fight. And how many would return home again at war's end?

Wynn finally broke the silence. "But

we've been sidetracked," he said to Henry. "You were speaking of a difficult assignment with the Force."

Henry stood again and moved to lean against the fireplace mantel. Just thinking of it brought deep, troubling memories. He could hardly bring himself to speak of it.

He looked over at his father, realizing he would have to talk about it. "Do you know what my last official duty was before I left my post?"

His father's expression reflected deep empathy with the emotion in Henry's voice.

"I had to take word to a woman that her husband had been killed. It's not the first time. In fact, I guess the hardest part is that it opened up an old wound I had hoped was healed. It brought back all the horror of four years ago at my first posting. The first time I had to deal with a death. It was a robust-looking young Swedish logger. His company reported he didn't come in with the crew at the end of the day. I found him— pinned under a fallen tree. Crushed."

Henry stopped a moment and shook his head. "I thought I had finally worked it through. The faces didn't haunt my days— my nights—like they once had, though I'll admit I still thought about it. But this new incident—this time an older trapper—brought it all back. The nightmares. The haunting memories. Finding that young logger was bad enough. But taking word to his widow—that was the hardest thing I have ever done in my life. I remember it all like it was yesterday."

The older man nodded in understanding.

The son began to pace again, the anguish in his heart nearly overwhelming him. He appreciated the fact that his father did not try to fill the silence with solicitous, empty words. This was something Henry would have to work through on his own.

"When I arrived, she ran out from the little cabin as soon as she heard my team approaching. She thought he was coming home. The minute she saw me—the uniform—her face went pale. She looked so . . . so lost, so broken. I thought she would faint before she even heard my message."

He whirled around to look intently at his father. "She was little more than a girl," he said, his voice full of his anguish, one hand thumping gently but firmly into the palm of the other. "Just a girl. Way up there in some logger's cabin. All by herself. She . . ."

He made an effort to calm himself, but

31

his chin was trembling.

"I . . . I suggested to her that we go back inside. A cold wind was blowing and the temperature—she would have suffered frostbite in no time and would have never even realized it. She let me lead her by the arm. By then she was already staggering. I'm sure she knew what I was going to say. She just kept repeating his name over and over in a . . . a little whimper.

"I tried to lead her to a chair, but she refused to sit down and . . ."

For a long moment he could not go on. The room was silent except for the crackling of the fire and the sympathetic whine of the dog.

He swallowed. "After I told her, she just sort of went to pieces. She clung to me and sobbed and sobbed. I have never heard such . . . such absolute heartbreak in all my life. An animal caught in a trap doesn't make such a pitiful sound. And she hung on. Just grabbed my jacket like she was drowning. I don't know how long I held her, praying silently, trying somehow to . . . to calm her . . . to ease her terrible pain. Dad, I've never felt so . . . so totally helpless in my entire life."

He lowered himself to the chair again

and stared into the fire, his jaw working as he fought to control his deep emotions.

"But that wasn't the worst of it," he finally went on. "I had just managed to calm her somewhat when . . . when I heard a new cry. She had a baby. Not more than a few months old. I wanted to run. To get out of there. And at the same time I knew I couldn't leave. I couldn't. But I didn't know what to do with them. How to help them."

He stood to pace again. The dog rose with him, his eyes passing from one to the other as though wanting to do something about the heaviness in the room.

"But when the baby cried—she suddenly changed. She immediately was rational. All . . . all mother. Like she knew she was needed. She passed that . . . that little one to me while she went for dry diapers. I'd never held a baby before. And he just lay there in my arms and looked up at me. I felt like weeping. I had just come to bring the news that his daddy had been killed . . . and he looked up at me and smiled. I felt like . . . like some kind of traitor."

He brushed at his lip again, agitation causing his usually broad shoulders to droop.

"She came back, and I asked her what I

should do. What she would do. She told me to go over and get her neighbor, Mrs. McKinnon. I didn't know if I should leave her alone, but I knew I couldn't just stay. Nor could I leave. Someone had to be there with her. I looked at her and the way she was holding the baby and decided it was the only thing I could do. Go for Mrs. McKinnon and pray that the woman—whoever she was—would come.

"I didn't know how long it might take. I made sure she had lots of wood for the fire, and I . . ." He hesitated and flushed slightly. "I sneaked the man's rifle out of the house. She had been so distraught I didn't want to take any chances. Then I headed for the McKinnons'. The woman agreed to go on over—without question. I was going to escort her back, but he—her husband—said he'd take her over. He was a big, burly fella. I figured the two of them, being neighbors, would be in a better position to help the young woman than I was."

Silence again.

The older man was the first to speak. "And that was the last you saw of her?"

Henry nodded.

"So you don't know—?"

"I've no idea."

"Surely the McKinnons—somebody— would have seen to her."

He shrugged his shoulders.

"What about the body? The young logger?"

"The logging company was looking after the details. I was off the case."

"They'd see that she was cared for. When you get back—if you are still worried, you can check—"

"I'm not going back. I got my new posting just before I left. They are sending me down south for a while."

"South? How do you feel about that?"

He shrugged again, trying to sound nonchalant. "It'll be a change." He sighed deeply, then continued, "Although I understand they are still struggling to survive the drought. A number of the farmers have given up. Moved on—or out. Others are barely hanging on. It's been tough." Thoughtful silence followed. "It'll be a change."

Henry leaned over to throw another log on the fire. Bright sparks sprinkled over the grate, popping like miniature firecrackers.

"But you can't get her off your mind." It was not a question.

Henry merely nodded his head. "I pray

35

that she was properly cared for," he said, "that the logging company did their duty. But that doesn't take away my—I don't even know how to put it into words, Dad—but I've never been so affected by grief—tragedy—before. Duty. Duty isn't enough at a time like that. You see another person so . . . so crushed, and there is nothing—*nothing*—you can do to ease the pain. To just walk into a life with such tragic news and then not do anything to help . . ."

He found no more words.

The older man stood, lifting himself from the chair with his strong arms to give support to the leg that could no longer do its job alone. He stepped forward to join his son before the fire, and for several minutes they stood shoulder to shoulder watching the flames devour the rich pinewood.

"Son, have you considered the fact that you *did* help?"

The younger man's head swung around. "I did nothing. Just . . . just left her and—"

"No. No, you didn't. You . . . held her. That was what she needed . . . at the time. Just someone to be there. To hold her while she wept. And you prayed."

He turned slightly, and Henry stared

into the familiar face nearly level with his own.

"And, Henry, if I'm not mistaken, you haven't stopped praying. Have you?"

Henry almost lost control, and he brushed at tears. Perhaps it was unprofessional for a member of the Royal Canadian Mounted Police to cry. But even a law officer was human.

Slowly he shook his head. "No," he admitted honestly. "No . . . I haven't stopped praying."

"When is Chrissie's train due in?"

Elizabeth lifted her head to look at her son. She was much relieved that after the talk he'd had with his father, he seemed to be more relaxed, even though his dark eyes still carried shadows. She was anxious for the opportunity to talk with Wynn to discover what it was that had Henry so troubled. Now she answered evenly, her words deliberately kept light. "Tomorrow. Five-o'clock train."

"She's liking her job?"

Is Henry merely trying to make conversation? Elizabeth wondered as she cast a quick look his way again.

No. Henry was genuinely interested. She could read him easily. She heard Wynn's chuckle. "She seems to have settled in easily enough—after a rather trying beginning."

Henry had already heard the story of Christine's unfortunate encounter and unwelcome ride home in the same motorcar that had caused the disaster.

"Does she see much of the boss's son?" Henry asked.

"I suppose she does from time to time," Elizabeth answered. "I think she has forgiven him. In a way she feels a bit sorry for him. He lost his mother when he was young, and it seems his father has the mistaken idea that as long as he gives the boy lots of expensive toys, including that motorcar, he's being a good father."

Henry shook his head. "I've seen a few of those around. It doesn't work."

"She had a bit of a struggle getting used to the secretary pool. A true pecking order. For a while she was always being put in her place. It didn't help matters any when Mr. Kingsley started requesting her in place of the young lady who had been at the top of the pack. Miss Stout had to intervene a time or two. Christine was about ready to quit.

The boss got wind of it and gave her an unexpected raise. That just added fuel to the fire."

"Things any better now?"

"I think things have settled down. Miss Stout apparently had a long talk with Mr. Kingsley. Told him just how things were for Christine. He's eased off. Said he'd let her work her way up. She's much more comfortable now."

Henry nodded. "I can't wait to see her," he said, rubbing his hands together.

Elizabeth thought back over the years. Henry had always been Christine's champion. Even when she had come to their home as a skinny, shy four-year-old, Henry had taken seriously his role of big brother. He'd been almost fourteen at the time. They had just managed to secure the legal documents that declared Henry as their own. What a day of celebration that had been. And then came Christine. Orphaned, rather than abandoned as Henry had been. And Henry had taken to her immediately. Right away she became "my little sister," and he protected her with an intensity Elizabeth had not seen in him before. Even his teasing of her had included a gentleness and care that made it fun for her too.

Just thinking of those days brought Elizabeth pleasure. Theirs had been a family so securely surrounded in love.

"You'll notice a difference," Wynn was saying, his tone now more serious. "She's not the little kid sister anymore. She's quite a young lady."

Elizabeth was proud of her children. Would not have wished for things to be any different. She and Wynn had raised them carefully, tenderly, preparing them to make their way in an adult world. But my, how she missed them. Still missed them. The house felt so empty at times. The joyous memories were bittersweet.

She was so sorry she had not been able to go with Wynn and Christine to get her settled in the city. There was no one else to stay with their elderly neighbor who had managed to break her leg at just the "wrong" time. Christine had understood, but it had not eased Elizabeth's disappointment at missing this important step in her daughter's life.

Henry's eyes now had that distant shadow in them. *What have we said?* Elizabeth wondered. She lifted her gaze to meet Wynn's, reading the question in his face as well. He shrugged slightly. They would talk, but now was not the time.

"She's about the same age as . . ." But Henry did not finish the murmured sentence. Elizabeth was puzzled, but she could tell by Wynn's face that he probably knew the rest. Something had happened in the North that had their young Mountie deeply troubled. Elizabeth must learn soon what was bothering their son.

CHAPTER 3

"We've been talking enough about me. What about you?"

The Delaney four were sitting before the open fire, mugs of hot chocolate in their hands, laughter filling the room as it had their lives. Christine, from her favorite spot on the rug, had been telling of the strangeness of city life and the unusual people she had met over the seven months she had been on her own. Her parents and brother had been content to listen, enjoying every minute of her lively accounts. But now she paused and looked up at her older brother, inviting him by her expression to share some stories of his own adventures.

He stirred a bit restlessly, and though he obviously was trying to keep the spirit of the evening, Elizabeth saw the underlying tension.

His grin seemed forced, but his tone was light. "My experiences haven't been as hilarious as yours, I assure you," said Henry, and he reached out to ruffle his sister's dark curls. Elizabeth wondered if Christine, with her sensitivity to her brother's moods, would catch the tension he was attempting to cover.

"We've had enough hilarious," insisted Christine. "Tell me about the North. I've missed it so."

A melancholy suddenly filled her voice. It was then that Elizabeth realized just how far from her roots Christine had been taken.

Christine brought her knees up and hugged them, her head bent forward so her long dark hair framed her face. She continued, nostalgia making her words sound plaintive, "Do the northern lights still put on a color-dance in the sky? Does the snow still crunch beneath your moccasins? Does the timber wolf still reign as king of the forest? Do the mornings still sing with the newness of life?"

Elizabeth could not see her face, but she could read in her voice the longing, the loneliness. What had it really been like for this wilderness girl to be consigned to the city? It had been her own choice, Elizabeth reminded herself.

"I think you should go back—and see," Henry answered.

Christine straightened her shoulders and shook her head. "There's no going back," she said, and her voice sounded both strong and resigned. "The world moves forward—not backward. What was—is no more."

How did we ever get onto this morbid train of thought? wondered Elizabeth. *Just a moment ago we were all bent over in laughter.*

Christine was continuing. "I may not be brilliant—but I've figured out that much. There's no use longing for what used to be. I can't be a little girl curled up in Mommy's lap enjoying a bedtime story. I can't run down the dusty track to meet my daddy as he comes home, his outline washed with colors of the setting sun. I can't sneak into your room in the middle of the night when I've had a bad dream and share your pillow. I can't play in the puddles with Tina or Mary Daw or Little Deer after a summer rain, or sit and watch you fish in the deep pool of the beaver dam. I can't romp with pups or take Kip for a—"

"Hey," Henry's words stopped her as he placed a hand on her head. "Of course you can."

She began to shake her head, tears now glistening in the corners of her hazel eyes.

"You can," Henry insisted. "You just did."

She looked puzzled.

"We've got all those memories," Henry explained. "Our wonderful growing-up years. Our family. Our friends. They stay with us."

"It's not the same," said Christine wistfully. "Sometimes I just ache to . . . to go back. To walk the trails through the woods. To smell the smoke from the campfires. To hear the soft music of the native tongue. I do miss it."

"Is that really what you miss—or childhood? I mean, it seems to me if one has had a great childhood—no matter where you live, what you experience—it's hard to let it go."

Elizabeth thought back to Henry's earliest years. His had not been a great childhood. His roving, lawless, and indifferent family had moved him from pillar to post, quarreling and growling all the way. Had Henry been able to erase those memories?

"Now, I didn't get me too great a start," Henry was saying. "I had family—lots of family. But we didn't think of one another as family. Not with caring. It wasn't until Dad and Mom took me in that I really felt at home. And you—do you remember back? Before you came to us? I still remember the day Dad brought you home. 'Elizabeth,' he said, 'do you think you have room for another one?' And she did. We all did. That's when I felt we were really a family. After you came." The smile the two exchanged moved Elizabeth more than she could have explained.

"Mom had told me about Susie and Samuel," Henry went on. "I always grieved inside. They were more real to me than my own brothers and sisters. More . . . a part of the family. Then there was little Louis. But he was so sickly when he came that he scarcely had the breath to cry. Even Mom's fussing and Dad's medicine couldn't keep him with us for long. I felt I had lost family. I felt sorrow. Real sorrow. Like a piece of the family was missing. And then you came. That's what I think of when I think back. When I want memories of growing-up years. Not the northern lights, not the winter snows, not the dogs we've played with.

Not even our many friends. I think of family. And I know inside that no matter where we would have lived, I would have good memories because of that."

Christine sniffed. Wynn passed her his handkerchief.

Elizabeth was busy with a hankie of her own. Henry's words were the most beautiful Christmas gift she had ever been given.

Christine nodded and even managed a smile. "You are right—as usual. We have been blessed." She struggled for composure and moved to lean against Henry's long legs. He placed a hand on her shoulder. Elizabeth could see his fingers curl in a little squeeze.

"I guess that's why I feel so sorry for someone like . . . like Boyd" were Christine's next words. "He has been so . . . impoverished. All he has ever had is . . . things."

"He's the only child?" asked Wynn.

Christine nodded.

"What's he like?" prompted Henry.

"Well . . . he makes all of the typists swoon," began Christine, and the little group all laughed again. "Trouble is, he is well aware of the fact. I think he loves the attention."

"So he's nice looking?" asked Elizabeth.

"*More* than nice looking," Christine answered with emphasis.

"I knew a young man like that once," said Elizabeth with a knowing smile toward Wynn. "Nice thing was, he didn't seem to be aware of it."

Christine and Henry understood the words and both sets of eyes turned to their father. "Oh, Boyd isn't *quite* as handsome as Dad," put in Christine, and more soft laughter filled the room.

"So what have his good looks done for him? Or to him?" asked Henry pointedly.

"He's . . . cocky. I've never quite figured out if he really feels that self-assured . . . or . . . or uncertain. But if he does feel insecure, he sure does a great job of hiding it." She chuckled, but there didn't seem to be much joy in it.

"After he splashed me so thoroughly—you heard about that?" She half turned to Henry, who nodded. "Well, I had little choice but to accept the ride home. It started out pretty . . . stiff. I was still miffed . . . but he seemed amused. That made me even angrier. But—in a way—he *was* a gentleman, though he never did get around to an apology. The next morning there was this big, lovely bouquet of flowers on my desk, and the card read, 'From the fool driver'—like it was a joke. I wasn't sure how to take it but finally just shrugged it off. I decided that city folks were different than country folks and that—in his own way—this was his apology."

"How old is this guy?" Again the query from Henry.

"Umm . . . not sure. Twenty-two, maybe."

"Does he have a job?"

"No. He's still going to school." Christine would not have said so, but she was rather relieved, and some disappointed, that Boyd had gone off to school. More and more his eyes had turned her way when he visited his father's office. It unsettled yet excited her. And when he began to hang around her desk and find little excuses to chat, she felt at times that she could scarcely breathe. She needed time—space—in order to sort out the reason for her skipped heartbeats.

"Where?"

Her attention turned back to the family who shared the room and the fire. "University. In the East. Toronto, I think."

Wynn stirred. "What's he studying?" he asked.

"I'm not sure. I don't know if he's sure. I think from what his father has said, he's changed his mind a couple times."

Elizabeth looked across at her husband and silently shared his concern.

"Any church background?"

Christine shifted her position and looked from one parent to the other. "None whatever," she replied. "Mr. Kingsley has little use for the church—or for God. I think he's angry that his wife died. Anyway, I doubt Boyd has ever been to church in his life. Not even to Sunday school. He believes church is for wackos."

"Wackos?"

"His words—not mine."

Elizabeth saw Wynn's eyes lift to the wall clock. "Speaking of church," he said, "if we are going to be on time for the Christmas Eve service, we'd best get ourselves on the move. Wouldn't want the rest of the wackos to start without us."

A good-natured chuckle rippled around the room. Elizabeth smiled contentedly. It was time to be up and out. She had been so looking forward to sharing a pew with her son and daughter again. Perhaps that was when she missed them the most. When they gathered for worship and part of her family was not there.

———————

"Why don't you two take Teeko for a walk?" suggested Wynn.

The gifts had been opened, the clutter cleared away, and the traditional Delaney Christmas breakfast of poached egg on toast had disappeared. From the kitchen came the aroma of the roasting turkey. Already the blueberry pie had been lifted from the oven, but it would be some time yet before they sat down again to the table.

Henry stretched long arms above his tall frame. "It would be good to work out a few kinks," he agreed. Christine hung up the dish towel. "Only if Mom promises to take a break while we're gone."

Elizabeth chuckled. "I promise. I was looking for an excuse for a second cup of coffee."

"What about it, big guy?" Henry asked the yawning dog. "Are you up for a tramp through the woods?"

The dog responded only with a thump of his tail, his recognition of having been spoken to. Henry then changed to "Teeko.

Walk?" At once Teeko was on his feet, his whole body shivering in anticipation as he headed for the door that led them outside.

"Guess he's willing," noted Henry.

"He's always willing," laughed Elizabeth. "Rain or shine. Day or night."

It didn't take them long to gather coats and mittens, and soon the house was quiet again. Elizabeth poured two cups of coffee and joined Wynn before the fire. She sipped quietly for a moment before she turned to her husband. "So . . . which one of our children should we be most concerned about?"

Wynn looked over at her but did not speak.

"Henry and his painful memory—or Christine with her pain of empathy?" she continued.

"I guess we didn't raise them to be insensitive," replied Wynn slowly. "But they do seem to be taking on others' burdens with perhaps too much intensity."

Elizabeth put down her cup. "It's hard," she mused. "So hard—in life—to arrive at that proper balance." She was thoughtful for a few moments before saying, "I do hope that Christine's compassion doesn't blind her to other things."

"You see the possibility of something more?"

Elizabeth nodded. "Sometimes the 'something more' sneaks up on one."

"You don't want her falling for this young man."

"No. No, I don't. I will be honest about it. It sounds risky to me. She knows the importance of a shared faith with the man she learns to love. His . . . his unawareness of spiritual things, of God, frightens me. But Christine knows all that. She knows about love. Respect. Goodness. She'll know better than to get involved—unless he changes. But—even then . . ." Her voice drifted to a halt before picking up the thought again. "If the feeling is . . . is pity because of what he didn't have, or guilt because of what she *did* have—then no. No. I don't want that kind of a relationship for her. She should have something much better than that."

"Will you tell her?"

Elizabeth shook her head. "I don't know. Perhaps. I'll need to . . . to pray about it. To feel . . . led."

He nodded.

"But our Henry—I've no idea how to . . . to help Henry."

"I know how he feels. At least to some

53

extent. A sudden death is always hard. And to be the bearer of the news is heart wrenching. I've had to do it a number of times over the years. But never . . . never to a young woman with an infant. It must have been an awful experience."

"Do you think . . . he'll be able to get over it?"

"Do we want him to?" Wynn looked directly into Elizabeth's eyes. When she didn't speak, he continued, "Time will help. But the experience will change him. In some way. If it is shrugged off, thinking 'that's their problem,' one becomes callous. Indifferent. If you let it stay with you, festering like an inner canker when there is nothing you can do about it, it brings cynicism. If you do what you can, accept it as part of life, but let God keep you open to others— then you grow from the experience."

Elizabeth nodded. She had always wanted her children to grow. To mature. To get beyond the selfishness of childhood and be able to reach out to others in a world full of sorrow and tragedy. But sometimes that growth came through such pain. Her mother's heart wished there were some other way.

"How do you think the folks are doing?" Christine asked as soon as they were a comfortable distance from the small house. Henry moved on a few steps, listening to the crunch beneath his heavy boots before answering. Like Christine, he would miss the sound of the snow underfoot if it were to be taken from him.

"Look all right to me," he answered lightly. "You?"

When she was slow in responding, he turned to look at his sister. "Okay," she said at length. "I think Mom looks a little tired."

"She always gets too involved in things. That's Mom. No wonder she's tired."

Teeko ran ahead, barking joyously at being outside. He turned once and looked back to make sure they were still following.

"Dad said anything about his leg?"

Henry shrugged. "You know he doesn't talk about it." Wynn never made mention of his injured leg.

"It still makes me angry when I think of it," Christine burst out. "He likes to shrug it off as being part of the job—but it isn't. At least, it shouldn't be. Just because he's a Mountie doesn't mean he should have to lose a leg to maintain law and order."

"What should he have done?"

"He saw the guy had a knife—and he knew he would use it."

"Are you saying he should have shot the fellow?"

It was Christine's turn to shrug. "I don't know. I've never been able to sort it out. But it doesn't seem right that he couldn't protect himself. That crazed idiot would have cut him up into little pieces if he'd been able—"

"He was drunk."

"Drunk or sober—what's the difference? Dad still lost his leg."

"Well . . . not totally. He's always saying how thankful he is that he still has it."

Henry thought back to the awful day of the incident. They'd been sure they were going to lose their father. When that fear was finally put to rest, they were sure he would at least lose the leg. But that didn't happen either. He'd been pulled from the North where he loved to work and had been given an office job instead, but he could still walk, although with a limp. They had all thanked God for that many times.

"Does he really hate being caged behind a desk instead of being out in the air and sun?" Christine wondered aloud.

Henry laughed. "Last time he talked to me he didn't sound at all envious. Said he was getting a bit old to enjoy nights huddled in blankets in a bank of snow, or trekking forty miles behind a dog team to check on some trapper's line."

"I think it's a bluff," said Christine.

Just then Teeko managed to flush a partridge. He set off at a run, barking at the bird winging its way above his head.

"Silly old dog would chase anything," laughed Henry. "Never knows when he's licked."

Christine smiled but made no comment.

"So . . . this here Boyd guy," ventured Henry, "you been out with him?"

Christine swung around to face him. "You mean—on a date?"

"Yeah."

She shook her head vigorously. "Not me. He scares me."

"Scares you? In what way?"

Christine quickly said, "Well . . . not scares me. But . . . I don't know. He . . . he sort of has a dark side. I haven't figured it out yet."

"Is he angry? Violent?"

"Oh no. Nothing like that. At least not that I've seen. 'Course I haven't been around him much. Just a . . . a closed-away feeling I get sometimes. Brooding. I don't know."

"Has he . . . asked you for a date?"

Christine hesitated. "Not really."

"Not really? Come on, Chrissie—yes or no."

Christine turned away, kicking at a clump of snow-covered grass as she passed by. "No," she said with more force than needed. "No—he has not asked me for a date."

Henry was not to be so easily put off. "But . . ." he prompted.

She turned back to him again. He'd always had a way of pulling forth her thoughts. Her feelings. But this time she seemed closed away herself as she said carefully, "I don't know. I sort of . . . sort of get the feeling that he has thought about it. That he might . . . if I gave any encouragement." She turned to walk on.

"And you haven't given encouragement?"

"No," she answered over her shoulder.

"Why?"

She stopped and faced him. "I'm not sure," she said, now sounding more forthright. "I've thought about it. I'd love to invite him to church. I worry about his attitude. He needs fixing—and that's for sure. But I don't know if I'm the one—if there is anything . . ." She paused, then burst out, "I wish you could meet him. You'd know what to do. There's just something about him that . . . disturbs me. But I can't just walk away, can I? What if—?"

Henry reached out and drew her close. "I trust you, Chrissie," he whispered softly. "If you . . . if you are unsure . . . then keep out of it. Stay away. Don't let him fool you into . . ." He did not complete the thought. He was sure his beloved sister understood his words and his feelings.

CHAPTER 4

Christine had difficulty getting back into the rhythm of city life. After the joys of once again walking in snowy white fields and along frosted trails, after spending long evenings before a warming fire with a favorite book and the peaceful security of family, she felt the city to be harsh and demanding. Trolleys clanged. Auto horns blared. Streets sloshed with muck after every snowfall. Christine had to adjust to the city environment all over again.

It did help some that she now knew her workmates—though certainly in a different way than she knew her childhood friends. There were a host of acquaintances right in her own office building—women who worked at desks close enough to touch, men who entered each morning and took their places through doors down the hall—the majority of whom she would not have thought of claiming as friends. She nodded to them when she arrived at her station in the morning. She exchanged courteous words throughout the day when her duties demanded it. At the end of the day she watched them shrug into their respective coats and turn back to the streets. She did not know where their homeward steps led them—nor did she particularly care. They were simply people who occupied a little space in her environs for a few hours of her day.

But there was one girl in the office who did capture Christine's interest as more than a casual acquaintance. They were about the same age. Though they were nothing alike in looks or temperament, Christine felt drawn to her. Jayne Easton had come from the farm. Christine felt sure Jayne was as out of her element in the city as was Christine herself. The young woman was not a plain Jane. Not by any means. In fact, her flaxen head of curls and her bright china blue eyes turned many heads for a second look. But Jayne seemed to be totally unaware of the attention she drew. She was quiet and withdrawn and seemed to be very unsure of herself. For some reason Christine could not define, she felt the need to shelter, to protect, the girl. She found herself making an effort to establish a relationship.

"How long have you been in the city?" she began as they munched their sandwiches in the lunchroom.

"Eight months, one week, and two days," replied Jayne.

Christine smiled. She had not kept such an accurate account.

"Where are you from?"

"A little community about seventy miles west."

"You miss it?"

The blue eyes shadowed. "Oh brother, do I ever."

"So why did you leave?"

She stirred restlessly and dropped her eyes. "Wasn't a job there."

Christine thought she heard a catch in Jayne's voice and felt the girl needed some time to regain her composure. She picked up her apple and took a bite.

Jayne eventually explained, "The folks needed help with medical bills. I've a little brother who hasn't been well. You don't make a lot of money on the farm. Pop always says it's a wonderful place to live—but that's all you get to do, just live. If it wasn't for the big garden, the chickens and all, I'm not sure one could even do that."

Christine felt her heart go out to Jayne.

"Is there just your little brother?"

"There are seven of us. The oldest two are married. Then there's me. Four younger."

"That's a big family."

She nodded.

"I just have one brother," volunteered Christine, then added, her voice full of feeling, "He's wonderful. Almost ten years older than me."

"Did your mother have other—?"

"I'm adopted. We both are." Christine's words sounded a bit abrupt. She hadn't intended them that way. She hurried on. "Our folks always wanted a family—so they took in kids whenever they found opportunity. First Mom took Susie—for a short while when her mother was ill—but as soon as the mother improved, they moved away and took Susie with them. Mom still keeps in touch with her, though. Mostly at Christmastime now. She's grown up. Has kids of her own.

"Then there was Samuel. They thought

they were going to get to keep him when his mother died and his father brought him to them. But the man remarried and came back for his son. It nearly broke my mother's heart. She still cries when she talks about it. She has no idea where he is now.

"Then came Henry. He was just—sort of abandoned by his family. It took Dad years to finally track them down and be able to arrange for legal custody of Henry. Henry says he was scared every day that they'd come back for him. My family really had a party when the papers finally came through.

"Then they had a little baby, Louis, whose parents were sick and stranded in a cabin in the North. By the time Dad found them, they were all too weak to move. In fact, the mother had already died. The father died soon after. Dad bundled up the baby and took him home in the front of his parka. But it was too late. He lived only for a short time. Henry remembers him.

"I was the next one. I lost my folks in a cabin fire. They managed to push me out the window into a snowbank. The window was too small for them to squeeze through. Dad took me home. It was several months before he was able to track down kin and get things finalized for my adoption. When it arrived, Henry wanted another celebration. So we did."

Jayne had been listening to every word, a shocked expression on her face. When Christine stopped, the other girl shuddered. "That's . . . that's horrible."

"They've been wonderful parents," Christine defended. "I feel so—"

"No, not that. The . . . the tragedies. The sickness . . . and fire."

"That's all part of the North," said Christine frankly.

"You lived there?"

"For most of my life."

"Where in the North?"

"Various places. The RCMP doesn't leave a man at one posting too long. When one is an officer, it's almost as dangerous to make friends as it is to make enemies."

"What do you mean?"

"An officer has to uphold the law and bring lawbreakers to justice. That's harder to do if one's personal friends are involved."

"I suppose," Jayne admitted.

"What's it like in the North?" Jayne queried after a moment.

"You mean the Indian villages? Or our cabins?"

"You lived in Indian villages?" The girl's eyes were wide now.

Christine merely nodded, taking another bite of her apple.

"Weren't you scared half to death?"

"Of what? Almost every man was armed. Besides, wolves and bears rarely came close enough to cause damage. A few dogs were raided when the food supply was low but—"

"I meant the Indians."

"Indians?" Christine did not understand the other girl's question. When it finally dawned on her what Jayne intended, she shook her head. "The Indians were my friends. My playmates. We were one big family. Oh, there were a few of them who could get out of hand, especially if someone brought in whiskey. But that happens here in the city among white people. For the most part I was welcomed into any home in the village. They all looked after me."

"Do you . . . do you speak Indian?" asked Jayne, sounding very much in awe of Christine.

"Cree. My father speaks it well, plus a bit of four or five other dialects. Mother speaks Cree—beautifully. Every once in a while we still speak it in our family—or sing it—just to hear it again."

"My," said Jayne, crumpling up the brown bag that had held her lunch. Looking directly at Christine, she asked, "Are you glad to be back?"

"Back? Oh, you mean in the city? I'm not . . . back. I'm *away*. Only now am I beginning to realize that I really am out of my element. Out of my community. Out of my homeland. Away from my people."

"You're not Indian, are you?"

"No. No, I'm a mixture of Scotch, French, and Irish. But I wish I were Indian. Then I would really belong there."

"My goodness," said Jayne again. "I thought I had a tough row to hoe. All I left was my family and . . ."

Christine's eyes prompted her to complete the sentence. When Jayne said nothing, Christine asked, "There's a special someone?"

Jayne blushed. "Not really," she answered. "I was . . . I was just hoping there would be. He'll forget all about me now. Likely already seeing Bessie Tellis," she finished, her voice low.

Christine again felt sorry for Jayne but thought that any comfort she might offer would seem trite.

"Is Henry Indian?" Jayne wondered.

"Hmm," she murmured, "I don't think I know Henry's roots—but, no, he isn't Indian."

"It must be—seem strange—not knowing your family. Mine is Swedish and German. Believe me, they never let one forget it. My father jokes about it all the time. If we're good, we're Swedes. If we're not, it's our German mother's fault." Jayne laughed, so Christine knew the teasing was all in fun.

Christine noticed the hour on the wall clock. It was time to get back to their desks. She was reluctant to close the conversation. Jayne was not nearly so shy when one had time to spend with her.

"Would you care to join me for church on Sunday?" Christine asked impulsively.

"Where do you go?"

"There's a little congregation that meets—"

"I'm Lutheran."

"Oh. No, this church isn't Lutheran."

"What is it?"

"I don't know . . . really. Just . . . just a little mission group. But they're great."

"I go to the Lutheran church on Forty-sixth Avenue. It's great too."

Christine was disappointed. It would be

so nice to be able to share the service with a friend.

"Maybe you'd like to come with me . . . sometime," ventured Jayne.

"Maybe . . . sometime." But Christine knew she would miss her own congregation if she went elsewhere. She supposed Jayne would too.

They were on their way back to their desks when Christine thought of something. "Easton doesn't sound Swedish," she said.

Jayne nodded in agreement. "My father was an orphan too," she said. "He took the name of the folks who raised him."

"Oh."

It seemed that the West had its share of splintered and restructured families.

———

Though the two girls did not attend one another's churches, they did develop a friendship. It was nice to have a real friend in the city, Christine decided, even though she rarely saw Jayne other than at work. Still, their lunch hours were shared, along with many thoughts and feelings about life.

For Christine the long evenings were spent mostly with books. If there was one thing about the city that she approved of, it

69

was the library. Christine made good use of it. Each Wednesday after work and again on Saturday morning, she made the trek to the big square building and exchanged her stack. Then she spent her evenings curled up in her small boardinghouse room, poring over the pages. It was her only escape to a bigger, more interesting world. *There are no prison walls if one has books*, she had read someplace. But even so, her days and nights often were lonely.

She had learned to like Mr. Kingsley in spite of his gruffness and his growl. She was convinced that under the rough exterior there was a heart that truly beat in tune with human kindness. The challenge was to find some way to unearth it. The big man seemed to treat her with favor. This did not sit well with Miss Stout, who, in Christine's opinion, nursed a secret, longtime crush on the boss.

Mr. Kingsley did not seem to notice Miss Stout's devotion, so the poor woman was viewed as merely efficient office help. Christine could not help but feel Miss Stout would have made a very good Mrs. Kingsley. Her primness and rigidity might have brought some order to the boss's rather chaotic life. On the other hand, his casual attitude and brashness might have loosened up the matron a bit. Christine was not the only one who had noticed more than passing interest on the part of his receptionist.

"Someone needs to do something," Christine mused one evening as she walked home after work. She was later than usual. Mr. Kingsley had called her into his office to discuss a typing project, and Miss Stout had hovered near the door on the pretext that she was anxious to close up shop and go home herself.

If I had my own place, Christine reasoned, *I would invite them both for supper.*

Well, she didn't have more than a single room, so there wasn't much she could do. Then a new thought hit her. *Mr. Kingsley does.* She had no idea where he lived or what it was like—but she'd find out. Perhaps with a bit of maneuvering, he would allow her to cook supper in his kitchen and invite the lady from the front desk. It was worth a try. She decided that she'd take the risk and ask.

The very next morning, she mustered up the courage to knock on Mr. Kingsley's door. "I was just thinking as I was going home last night," she began, "I would love to invite you and . . . and Miss Stout for supper. You've both been . . . so kind to me." She stopped for breath. He had raised his head, and she thought she saw a glimmer of interest under the bushy brows.

"I have only a small room. No . . . no cooking facilities." She thought she could detect a look of disappointment. "But I . . . wondered if you'd mind if I . . . if we used your home . . . for the meal. I'd purchase the ingredients and . . ." She drew to a stop. "Of course if it's an imposition—"

"No. No imposition. I've a kitchen. I never eat there. Always grab something at one place or another. Don't even know what's there. Cleaning lady is the only one who goes in there, and I've no idea what she does when she's there. But if you want to check it out, that'd be just fine. Yes, yes. Just fine. Haven't had a home-cooked meal since I don't know when. You can cook too?"

Christine wasn't sure what he meant by "too," but she nodded her head.

"That's great. Just great," he blustered on, rubbing his hands. "When would you like to do this?"

"Whenever it fits your schedule—and Miss Stout's."

"My schedule. My schedule isn't hard to fit—where meals are concerned. I've no idea about Miss Stout's calendar." He hesitated and rolled his pencil between two beefy fingers. "You sure you want Miss Stout? Isn't she a bit sour?"

"Oh yes—no. I mean—she's been very kind to me. I thought I could say a . . . a thank-you this way."

He nodded then, and Christine felt her heart skip. It seemed like her plan would work out. He gave her a lopsided grin and waved her out. "Check with Miss Stout," he said. "Any evening will suit me."

And so things were arranged, and on the following Friday night Christine found herself searching out 716 East Summit Avenue. She had taken the trolley—which was no small feat considering the grocery bags she carried with her.

Mr. Kingsley had given her the address and a general idea of where it was located, but when she found it she felt there must be some mistake. She stood on the sidewalk staring at an enormous house. Surely it was not a single-family dwelling. Christine's eyes roamed over the impressive structure in disbelief. Checking the address again, she finally made her way along the walk to the back door.

Letting herself in with the key her boss

had provided, she discovered the inside was even more breathtaking. Christine had never been in such a house before. Even the Calgary home of Uncle Jon and Aunt Mary could not compare with this one. There were crystal chandeliers, a winding oak staircase, heavy furniture polished to a deep shine, glistening mirrors, and carpets so thick they felt like forest moss. Christine slowly let out her breath.

But she hadn't come to stare, she reminded herself. She found the massive kitchen and began searching through cupboards for proper utensils. She had planned chicken and dumplings, mashed potatoes and gravy, buttered carrots and creamed turnips. Dessert would be a berry pie. It was not a fancy meal, but with any luck at all, it would be a tasty one. Unless, of course, she had selected a menu not to Mr. Kingsley's liking. Well, anyway, this was food she knew how to prepare, and she'd just hope for the best.

Christine's initial nervousness mostly disappeared as she immersed herself in the familiar routine. She almost chuckled aloud as she thought, *If Mama could see me now . . .*

By the time Miss Stout rang the front

doorbell, the aromas from the kitchen were penetrating the entire house. The china from the large breakfront was now arranged on the table in the big dining room. Christine thought it looked rather elegant. Much different from the Delaney supper table in the North.

Miss Stout came in rather stiffly, but she looked surprisingly chic in a new floral dress. Her eyes studied everything about her. Christine assumed this was the first time the woman had been in the house.

"I'm sure Mr. Kingsley would want you to make yourself at home," smiled Christine. "Everything is ready. I'll just need to dish up when he arrives."

"He's not here?" Her disappointment was obvious.

"I'm sure he will be soon. He told me he had a bit of work to finish up."

"That man. He works far too hard," murmured Miss Stout.

"I guess he feels he may as well work as to come home to this big empty house," observed Christine. She excused herself and hurried back to the kitchen to keep an eye on the supper.

It was not long until she heard voices in the living room and smiled softly. Mr.

Kingsley was home. He would finally notice Miss Stout as something other than an office fixture. She heard Miss Stout's nervous, high-pitched titter. *I'll just give them a few more minutes before I serve the food*, thought Christine. Her plan seemed to be working very well.

By the time she entered the living room to invite her two guests for supper, Mr. Kingsley seemed to be quite at ease. He sat near the open fire in a huge, well-used chair, legs crossed, fingers thumping out a little rhythm on the arm of the chair. He was even smiling.

"I hate to interrupt," began Christine, "but supper is served."

Mr. Kingsley was immediately on his feet. "I didn't know how much longer I could stand it," he said in his boisterous manner. "Those fumes—"

"Fumes," giggled Miss Stout. "Really, Mr. Kingsley. One does not speak of delicious food aromas as fumes." She giggled again.

He took no offense, and together they moved to the dining room in a jovial mood.

Christine saw them seated, then proceeded to serve up the dishes. She took her own meal in the kitchen, though she ate little because of her tension. Did they like the food? Were they getting on well?

Christine received high praise for the meal, almost to the point she felt embarrassed. She was glad when the last crumb of pie was eaten and her guests pushed back from the table.

"Never had a better meal," said Mr. Kingsley, wiping his mouth on the napkin. "Had forgotten what home-cooked food tasted like." He smacked his lips and tossed his napkin beside his plate.

"Why don't you have your coffee by the fire while I clean up?" suggested Christine.

"Oh, I must help," offered Miss Stout.

"I'll manage just fine," Christine quickly said, and Miss Stout did seem relieved. "It's all a part of the thank-you for your kindness."

Miss Stout beamed. "Well . . . if you insist. That's most kind." She gave Mr. Kingsley another big smile.

"We'll have that coffee," Mr. Kingsley said to Christine. "But you join us. The cleaning lady can take care of things."

"Oh no. I'd never cook a meal, make a mess, and leave it to someone else. It'll only take me a few minutes." She poured the coffee and withdrew, humming to herself as she went.

This was going even better than she had dared hope. Mr. Kingsley had been most amiable at the supper table, and Miss Stout had fairly glowed. Surely with a bit of prompting the two lonely people would realize that they could add much to one another's world.

CHAPTER 5

"Cupid's arrows don't always shoot straight." Her father's words came back to Christine the next morning as she entered the office. Miss Stout sat at her desk, her lips pursed as dourly as ever. But there was a new twinkle in her eyes and a new lacy handkerchief pinned to her normally unadorned navy suit. Christine knew her father's words meant that one should not attempt to play Cupid. Yet she could not keep from feeling a bit victorious as she hung up her coat and gave the receptionist a good-morning smile.

"Mr. Kingsley wants to see you," announced Miss Stout. "He said to send you in the moment you arrived." The twinkle in her eyes deepened. Christine nodded and went for her steno pad.

"Oh, I don't think you'll need that," said Miss Stout lightly.

Christine's brow knit in puzzlement.

"I think it might be something . . . on a more personal basis," the woman explained, looking flushed.

Christine clung to the steno pad and moved slowly toward the door. She had not felt such nerves since the first time she had stepped inside the big room.

She rapped lightly. "It's open" came the gruff invitation. She proceeded in, the pad clutched in two hands.

"Miss Stout said—" But she got no further.

"Sit down. Sit down," he said loudly, waving the stub of a pencil he held between two fingers. A broad grin spread across his face.

She was not used to being greeted by her boss in such fashion. She sat in the chair he had indicated, pencil and pad poised.

"That was a great supper last night. A great supper."

Christine managed a nod in acknowledgment of his compliment.

"I thought about it all night. Well—most all night." He chuckled deep in his throat. Christine had not heard him attempt to laugh. "It's a long time since I've had a meal like that. Boyd—he must have missed them too. Says the cafeteria food at the university isn't any improvement over the local greasy spoon." He laughed again. Christine decided she preferred his gruff, all-business attitude to this jovial, overly familiar one.

He leaned back and looked at her, his chair squeaking beneath his weight. He grinned again and toyed with the pencil in his fingers.

"Well—I finally got it all figured out. You're in a little boardinghouse room. Right?"

Christine, perplexed, nodded slowly.

"And I've got this great big house."

She had no idea where this conversation was heading. She simply stared back at him.

"And you're a good cook. Great cook."

She sat, mute, her cheeks warming with embarrassment.

"And I've been living on bacon fat and strong coffee."

He waited expectantly. She had no idea what to say. What to think.

He leaned forward again, the chair groaning in protest.

"Don't you see? It's a perfect match."

Christine shook her head. "I'm . . . I'm

afraid I don't . . . I'm not following you, sir."

"Hey—I thought we got rid of that 'sir' stuff long ago," he chided. "Makes me feel as old as Methuselah." He shifted again and looked over at her. "It's simple. Don't know why I didn't think of it sooner. You move in with me."

Christine was beyond shock. She was sure she had misunderstood.

His beefy hand slapped down on his desk. "As cook," he said.

"But—"

His words spilled over her attempt to protest. "I've got all this room. You're paying room and board. You can take a room upstairs. Any room. You can have your pick of the bunch. There were five of 'em up there last time I counted. 'Course one is Boyd's. But you can have any others you want. You get your room and board in exchange for fixing my suppers."

Christine felt as if her body had turned to ice. What on earth—

"I'll pay the bills," he hurried on, as though to assure her that the arrangement would indeed be to her benefit. "All the bills."

"I . . . I don't . . ." she faltered. "It's . . ."

"It makes complete sense," he argued, sounding frustrated at her hesitance. "Why should you be shelling out money? Why should I be living on bacon and eggs? It's a perfect solution."

Christine was relieved she was sitting down. She tried to think. What could she say and not jeopardize her job? She had just been invited to share one of the most beautiful and auspicious dwellings in the entire city of Edmonton. But the circumstances . . . She was sure her mother and father would say, "Absolutely not!"

"I'll . . . I'll have to think about it." She clamped her lips on the "sir" that nearly slipped out.

"What's to think about? I can send Jesse round to pick up your things this evening. We can get right to it."

"But . . . how will folks . . . what will they think?"

He waved the pencil. "Who cares what they think?"

"I care . . . sir."

The man's face grew serious, as though he was actually trying to look at this through Christine's eyes. He studied her carefully for a few minutes. "Okay," he said at last, leaning forward and tapping his pencil on the wooden desk. "I see I went too fast. Let's go over this again."

He leaned back.

"I thought you liked to cook."

Christine nodded. She did enjoy the kitchen.

"You're paying for your little room."

She nodded again.

"But you don't like big houses?"

"Your house is . . ." Christine could not think of how to describe such an awesome dwelling. "It's lovely," she finally said lamely.

"So it's not the house?"

"Not at all, I just—"

"Is it me?"

"Sir, young women simply do not move in . . . move in with bachelor men," she managed, her tone growing more determined with each word.

At his frown, she hurried on. "It would be different—quite different if you had a wife."

"If I had a wife, I wouldn't need a cook," he growled.

Christine flushed.

"So what is your solution?" he demanded.

"I . . . I've no solution. I haven't even considered—"

"Well, consider it now."

"I'll . . . I'll have to think about it—pray about it. Talk to my folks."

"If it's just my being alone, Boyd will soon be home."

Christine shook her head. "I'm sure that would not fix it."

"Then bring someone with you. What about that . . . that Miss Easton? I've seen you talking with her. Bring her." He slapped the desktop and swore. "Bring the whole typing pool."

Christine rose to her feet on trembling legs and wondered if they would work well enough to take her from the room. "I'll . . . pray about it," she repeated through stiff lips and turned to go.

"Pray about it," she heard her boss mumble disgustedly to himself, but she did not turn back.

As she opened the door, Miss Stout looked up. Christine could feel the woman's eyes on her but refused to look her direction. *And you,* she fumed inwardly, annoyed, *I suppose you thought you'd be invited for supper every day of the week.*

Christine did pray about it. Honestly. On the one hand she realized how pleasant it would be to live in such an opulent home with so much room, along with the pleasure of spending time in the kitchen each night. She would be preparing meals for Mr. Kingsley and herself. Then Boyd when he returned home from school. She did not even consider Miss Stout as a dinner guest. As far as Christine was concerned, the woman deserved no more free suppers.

She wrote a letter to her parents telling them of Mr. Kingsley's proposal. She included the fact that he had said she could bring her friend Miss Easton along with her. *That would be fun,* she told herself as she penned the words. Built-in companionship in the big house. They could work together in the big kitchen. Read books before the library fire. There was even a player piano in the drawing room.

But each time Christine's enthusiasm began to grow, she felt an inner disquiet. *Abstain from all appearance of evil* came back to her mind as she sealed the envelope. And how would it change things at work? With diligence and care, she had finally earned her spot in the typing pool. She had now been accepted as skilled and hardworking, not "the boss's favorite." What if she moved into the boss's house? Would she be shunned all over again? Christine was certain she did not want that.

But to refuse. How would he take her decision? Would he be miffed? Downright angry? Might he terminate her employment? Christine continued to pray and anxiously checked her mail until the response from her folks arrived.

"This is a most unusual circumstance," her mother wrote. "We have talked about it at length and prayed about it many times. We have come to the conclusion that not knowing the man, nor the full implications of the situation, we must trust God to lead you to the right decision."

This was little comfort to Christine. She appreciated her parents' faith in her, but she wished they had made the decision for her. Mr. Kingsley was waiting for her decision. Boyd was soon due back from the university. She knew she had to decide one way or the other. But what was right? She had not brought it up with Jayne. She did not need the complication of pressure from another source. The week dragged by with Christine's heart nearly stopping every time Mr. Kingsley's office door opened. She knew she could not avoid the inevitable forever.

On Monday morning she slipped into her desk as uncertain as ever. Then she noticed Miss Stout grimly cleaning out Jayne's station.

"What—where's Jayne?" she asked.

"Foolish girl," Miss Stout said with tight lips. "She went home for the weekend. Phoned in this morning to say she would not be coming back. She's getting married to some . . . some country yokel. Never even gave proper notice."

Getting married. The words rang in Christine's ears. Jayne getting married. So her young man had not taken up with Bessie—whoever she was—after all. Jayne would be so happy. Christine could not help but smile.

Then came the realization that Jayne would no longer be available to share the big house. There was no one else in the typing pool she had any interest in asking to share the unusual arrangement. That meant it had been decided for her. Now she must not put it off any longer. She had to talk with Mr. Kingsley. She took a deep breath, squared her shoulders, and picked up her steno pad. She didn't expect to need it, but it was something to hang on to.

"Come," called the gruff voice when she rapped on the door.

Christine steeled herself and entered. "Mr. Kingsley?"

He lifted his head. "Ahh," he said, tossing aside his pencil. "You've finally finished praying."

Christine nodded.

"Didn't think God was ever going to answer," he went on with a sly grin.

Christine did not share his amusement.

"Sit down," he offered, waving toward a chair.

Christine did.

"I take it from your face that the answer is no."

She nodded dumbly.

He seemed to think about that for some time before he pushed away from his desk and rocked back in his chair.

"Just out of curiosity," he said, studying her face, "why wouldn't He let you? I mean—I had no ulterior motive—except a few good meals. You're young enough to be my daughter—surely He didn't think I'd have designs on you. If I wanted another wife, there are lots of them out there. So why not?"

"He didn't say—I mean . . . perhaps He did . . . in a way. I just couldn't feel comfortable about it. I know that . . . that your house is beautiful and your offer was out of kindness. But it . . . it just didn't feel . . . right. I don't think people would understand, and I didn't want . . . I couldn't risk possibly damaging the name of my parents—or my God—just to get something better . . . for me."

He seemed to think about what she had said, weighing it carefully. He reached out to pick up his pencil and began to roll it between finger and thumb. "So . . . you think my offer would be better for you."

"Oh yes," said Christine quickly. "You've such a beautiful home, and I could have cooked . . . anything. Everything. It would have . . ." But she stopped uncertainly. She did not want him to misunderstand. "I'm sorry," she finally stammered.

"I'm not." He began to tap the pencil. "I was afraid you scorned my offer. That you felt it insulting. That . . . that riled me a bit. But now I see that . . . well . . . that you made your decision for another reason. I don't share your views about God. But I can respect you for sticking to what you believe. I'm disappointed . . . of course. But . . ." He shrugged his massive shoulders and pulled his chair closer to his desk.

She knew she had just been dismissed.

"Miss Delaney," he called after her when she was almost to the door. "Should you ever change your mind . . ." He let the sentence drop. Christine gave a slight nod.

She had her hand on the doorknob when he called again. "And bring me in another pencil. This fool thing's worn down to the quick."

CHAPTER 6

The location of the detachment had not been chosen because it was a large or prominent prairie town. Its claim to an RCMP office was its central position in the area that needed to be patrolled. Amid miles and miles of stark prairie and more miles of empty foothills sat this little town, directly in the middle. The distances no longer had to be covered on horseback—though Henry knew there would be days during the winter when he would long once more for a good dog team and a sled. Many roads, in the best of weather, posed difficulty even for the high-built Fords. He dreaded the winter storms and spring rains. But they'd have to deal with those when the times came. For the moment it was enough to face and manage what came up day by day.

He rubbed at the tension in the back of his neck. Though it had been a routine day—which to a police officer was always an advantage—he still had reports to write up. He was hungry, but the thought of food at the local café did not entice him. Everything they served was so highly spiced it made his stomach complain. Rogers, his fellow officer, joked, "If it didn't taste like fire, it'd have no taste at all." But it was either settling for café fare or the impossible task of rustling up something in his bachelor quarters.

He had been at his new posting in the South for three weeks. Three weeks. It didn't sound long. Yet it felt like forever. It was so different from the North. He'd been watching and observing to catch the feel of the whole flow of life here from his two fellow officers. Even so, he felt he was constantly on the brink of making some major official faux pas. So far he had managed to cover his hesitancy and fear of going against what was culturally acceptable.

Canadian law was the law of the West. He would uphold the law as he had vowed and been trained to do. But the details—the things that swung on individual interpretation—were the issues that could stump him.

The Force had a reputation to uphold. An image to protect. Henry was very conscious of that fact. He lived and breathed with the Force in mind.

He rubbed his neck with more vigor. *I'm not sure I was cut out for this* ran relentlessly through his mind. He silently noted, *I feel I'm walking on a beaver dam in spring flood-water. I'm not quite sure where to place my next step.*

"Boy," he admitted aloud, feeling the fringe at the back of his head. "I've got to get a haircut."

Three weeks was too long to let the regulation cut go. But Henry had been so busy trying to figure out his new posting that he'd not had time to look up a barber.

He couldn't remember seeing a striped pole in this little one-horse town. Well, there must be somebody who cuts hair. He looked at the young constable across the room, busily scratching out his daily report.

"Laray," he asked. "Where does one get a haircut in this town?"

"Sam's," Laray answered without even looking up.

There was a stirring at the other desk in the room. Rogers repeated, "Sam's." Henry noticed the two officers exchange a look and a grin. *They are setting me up,* thought Henry. But he pretended to fall in with whatever their little scheme might be.

"He the best place in town?"

"Sam's," repeated Rogers. "Definitely."

"Only place in town," put in Laray with a chuckle.

"Wouldn't matter though—if there were a dozen. Sam's would still be the place to go," said Rogers. Now both laughed.

Do these guys think I'm dumb or what? thought Henry, but he only nodded and repeated, "Sam's."

With a final chuckle from his two companions, they all returned to their paper work. *Suppose Sam's is about on par with Jessie's Grill,* Henry mentally groused. *Tortured stomach—tortured hair.*

He shrugged and went back to his reports. The sooner he finished, the sooner he could get to Jessie's, down the spicy food, chase it with his mints for stomach acid, and head for bed. Tomorrow might be a totally nonroutine day. He needed sleep to handle whatever might come.

The three left the building together. Laray turned to lock the door behind them. "Going to Jessie's?"

"Where else?" This from Rogers.

Laray laughed. "Yeah—where else?"

They fell into step.

"Did you find that little church you were asking about?" Henry knew the question was directed to him.

"I did."

"So how's it going?"

"Fine. You might want to join us."

The other two men both laughed, and Laray said, "Not me. I was done with church when my pa wasn't able to whip me anymore."

"What's it like?" queried Rogers.

"Small. But friendly. I think I'll like it. I've gone only once. Drew Sunday duty on the other two weekends."

"I don't mind Sunday duty," put in Laray. "Often quieter on Sunday."

"Except for the guys who party too much on Saturday night," offered Rogers. "I get awfully tired of handling drunks and breaking up fights."

Henry had thoughts of his own on the subject, but he kept them to himself. They walked the remainder of the way in silence. Even the smell of Jessie's Grill was hot and spicy.

They were nodded to a table by Jessie. She came over herself, her grin revealing the missing tooth. Somehow in Jessie's face it seemed to fit. She was . . . well, she was rather rugged in appearance. Brassy red hair was pulled back from bony cheeks in a bedraggled hair ribbon. The bright red lipstick, applied somewhat carelessly, matched in tone the bright rouged spot on her sallow cheeks. Her strident voice seemed to match her looks.

Already, though, Henry had sensed that the people of the community had respect for Jessie. She'd had a tough go, but she wasn't looking for favors or handouts. She worked day and night, but she was making it on her own. Henry knew there must have been a Mr. Jessie somewhere in the past, though the only evidence of him now was the handful of little Jessies he'd spotted here and there. He had not asked questions about the family but expected to learn more in time. His eyes searched her face as she stood by their table. He felt sorry for the woman and her obviously difficult circumstances.

"What you got cooking tonight, Jessie?" asked Laray good-naturedly. There really wasn't need for the food-spattered menus she pushed toward them. The regulars had each item already memorized.

"Special is beef stew 'n bakin' powder biscuits," she said. She turned her head away to cough.

The stew would be nothing like his mother's, but Henry ordered it anyway.

"Make it two."

"Three."

While Jessie went to dish up, Henry stretched out his legs. "Either of you happen to know of a cheap place a fellow might rent? I might like to batch."

"Batch? Man, I'd hate that," said Laray. "I'd hate to eat my own cookin'."

"I think I'd hate to eat your cookin' too," joked Rogers.

Henry had other thoughts. He didn't mind cooking at all. Had almost enjoyed it while in the North, and he'd had precious little to cook with there. The nearby corner store here would make things much easier. Besides, he knew his own cooking would be much easier on his digestive system.

"Don't know of anything right off. If I hear of anything, I'll let you know," Rogers responded. "I know this guy in real estate. I'll ask him, if you'd like."

"I'd appreciate it," said Henry.

Their plates arrived. Other patrons came and went. Henry was very aware of eyes on the uniforms. One rough-looking cowboy glared at them. Probably had spent a night locked up for some infraction of the law. Others ducked their heads. A few young girls cast interested glances their way. Older women and town businessmen nodded in acknowledgment. The presence of the Force brought stability to towns like theirs.

Henry was only too glad to finish the stew. After his last drink of bitter coffee, he rose. "Might be a little late in the morning," he said, running a hand over his hair before placing his Stetson. "Gotta get this hair cut. Where do I find this fella Sam?"

"Sam's? Just off Main Street. Corner of Main and Fourth, second building south."

"What time does he start?"

Henry did not miss the exchange between the two other officers. "Eight-thirty."

"Thanks," said Henry with a nod. Already he was planning to be the first one in the door when Sam flipped his sign to Open.

But when he arrived at eight-fifteen, the chair already was occupied by a very young boy. Henry ruefully removed his Stetson and hung it on the hat rack. He hoped this would be worth the wait. If the other two got their hair cut by Sam, as they claimed, he should fare all right.

"Take a seat. I'll be right with you," a woman called. He'd never found a barbershop with a receptionist before.

He took a seat and picked up a day-old paper. The headlines announced conflict across the Atlantic, food lines and railroad hobos, more farms and businesses fighting for survival in the prairie dust bowl. Henry sighed and put the bad news down.

He heard a step and then the voice again. "Here you go. Give this to Mrs. Crane. She's going to the meat market and promised to get some sausage for Mommy."

The boy hopped down from his perch and disappeared through the back doorway.

"Now—run straight home."

Henry heard his giggle. "I'm not going home, Mom. I'm going to Mrs. Crane's house. Remember?"

There was laughter in the voice that responded. "I meant home to Mrs. Crane's. Here, kiss me 'bye."

He heard the little smack. "Now run."

Henry picked up the paper again. He did not want to intrude on this private moment.

"Bye, Mom," the child called as he

bounded out the door.

Henry concentrated on the paper as the woman entered the room. He should be next, providing Sam—probably her husband—was on site. She was arranging some tools on the small shelf near the barber chair. From the corner of his eye, he noticed her lift a black barber cape.

"You're next," she announced.

"I was . . . I was looking for Sam," he managed to croak out as he put the paper aside and stood.

"I'm Sam" came the voice from behind the cape.

He was totally taken aback. "You give haircuts?"

"That's what the sign says." Her tone was crisp.

He moved awkwardly toward the chair. "Just the standard regimental cut," he heard himself saying as he settled into it.

"I understand," she replied, her voice still cool. "I've done a good many cuts for the Force."

Of course. If she was the only barber in town, she had been giving the men their haircuts. "I guess you have," he mumbled. "Being the only barber here."

"Look," she replied stiffly, "you don't

like my haircut, you can drive into Fort Macleod."

He lifted his eyes to the large mirror reflecting the scene in the shop, and he saw her face for the first time. She was standing directly behind him, her hands holding the cape and her expression questioning whether to proceed or send him on his way.

"No. I didn't mean . . . sorry. Go ahead. Please."

Her hands swished the cape over his shoulders, and the woman leaned forward to fasten it firmly. He got his first full look at her face. A mass of curly brown hair framed an oval face with a slight dimple in one smooth cheek, and she had a pair of the loveliest violet eyes.

It was those eyes that confirmed the truth to him. He knew with a surety that sent his head—and heart—reeling. This was she. This was the young woman he had been sent to almost five years earlier. This was the Swedish logger's young widow.

Henry fought to control his swirling emotions. He was totally unprepared for this sudden encounter.

CHAPTER 7

Christine was thrilled to note the early signs of spring. Though dirty snow still lined the sidewalks where the sun's rays were unable to reach, the water trickling along in the gutters could almost sound like the streams in her beloved North country. She closed her eyes for a moment to enjoy the pleasant memory. *Well,* said Christine to herself, opening her eyes to continue her walk to work, *running water is running water. Even here in the street it still makes wonderful music.* She wondered if any workers hurrying along ahead of her had noticed the sound.

She clung to her especially light frame of mind as she, almost by habit, entered the big building, climbed the stairs, and turned to her right. The same routine, the same duties, the same Miss Stout faced her as she opened the office door. The woman had stopped wearing the lacy hankies and fancy pins on her lapels. Apparently she had again given up on Mr. Kingsley. Christine thought the receptionist carried her own little halo with her—not a halo of light but one of cloud. It drifted about her head and wrapped about her shoulders. *I am a lonely spinster,* it seemed to say. *I am unappreciated. Unloved.* Miss Stout on occasion withdrew even more deeply into her gloom and wrapped it about her thin body. Christine did hope this wouldn't be one of those days.

She did not have time to hang up her coat before Miss Stout said, "Mr. Kingsley wishes to speak with you." Her words were terse, and Christine could imagine that cloud being tucked in tightly.

"Thank you, Miss Stout," she answered brightly, hoping to share a bit of her spring happiness. She did not bother to go for her steno pad. If she needed it, she'd come back. None of the other girls had arrived yet, so there would be no observers of the early-morning visit to the boss's office.

She rapped on the door and opened it. "You wished to see me?"

The shaggy head swung her way. "You here already?"

Christine felt the query did not need a reply.

"Sit," the man said. She sat.

He pushed his chair back, then changed his mind and leaned forward. "I know your answer was no, and I'm not out to change that." At the same time he raised a hand to forestall any words she might be inclined to say. "However . . ." He hesitated. "I was wondering if you'd object to making another supper. Just one." He lifted the hand again, this time palm up.

Christine gave the matter thought, then nodded silently.

"Good."

He exhaled loudly and pushed back again, looking very pleased. Christine's immediate thoughts went to Miss Stout. The woman would be overjoyed.

"When?" she asked simply.

"Friday. This Friday. I'll do all the shopping—just give me a list."

"Friday." She nodded. "Fine. Is there anything in particular you'd like me to serve? I have little experience with any fancy dishes."

"Fancy dishes we don't need. Just some of that chicken and dumplings you served before. That was wonderful."

"But . . . but don't you think your guest might enjoy something . . . well, different this time?"

"Nope. Nope. He'll love that, I know he will."

He? Who was her boss referring to?

"It's to be a surprise. I haven't told him a thing about it."

Whatever the plan and whoever the guest, Mr. Kingsley seemed tremendously excited.

"How many? For supper?" asked Christine.

"Just us. Two. And you, of course. I want you to sit with us this time."

"Me?"

"I want it like . . . like a family meal. Instead of you serving like a maid."

Christine swallowed and nodded again. "If you wish."

He beamed. "That's all set, then. You just get me that list."

"What if I go ahead and get what I need and you simply reimburse me?"

"That's good. That's great. I never did like shopping." He sounded relieved.

Christine rose. "Friday," she said as she turned to the door.

"Friday," her boss agreed, obviously

very pleased with himself. "Oh," he called after her. "You can plan on the meal being ready about seven. Boyd won't be back home until then."

Christine nearly stopped in midstride. *Boyd?* So now she was to be cooking a meal for the boss's son. For some reason she could not have explained, her heart suddenly began to beat much faster.

Christine was in the large kitchen nervously fussing over the final preparations for the meal when Boyd arrived. She could hear Mr. Kingsley's booming voice welcoming his son home from college. It made her even more anxious. She wasn't sure she'd be able to keep her hands from trembling as she served.

"Boy, that's the longest trip . . ." Christine could not pick up the rest of Boyd's words. She heard both men laugh uproariously and wondered what the joke was. With a final flutter of nerves she picked up two filled serving bowls and proceeded to the dining room. Quickly her eyes scanned the table. She had tried hard to make the table setting attractive without being too feminine. She wondered now if it seemed overdone, a bit showy for two bachelors. Quickly she removed the two candles in their tall crystal holders. Still she was uncertain. The fanned napkins were the next to go. She shook them out, then folded them and laid them beside the plates. That helped—but she was sure her aunt Mary would have been disappointed.

She had lived with Uncle Jon and Aunt Mary in their Calgary home while she took the secretarial course. During that time she had begged to be taught the niceties of city life that would prepare her for being a hostess in an urban setting. Though her mother had taught her the accepted manners of genteel society, her upbringing in the North had placed her far beyond the range of city social customs. Aunt Mary had been happy to teach her the duties of a charming hostess, along with the decorative touches that helped to make a memorable meal. Christine had been put under Cook's tutelage in the kitchen. She had loved it. In fact at one point she had considered becoming a chef instead of continuing her secretarial training. Her practical nature had kept her on track, however. There were far more positions available for secretaries than for chefs.

Now she fidgeted with the cutlery and

rearranged the water glasses. Was the crystal too much?

She heard the voices drawing close and guessed that Mr. Kingsley was gradually leading his son toward the dining room. There was no more time for fussing. She reached up to tuck a stray curl away, and then they were in the doorway. Mr. Kingsley pushed his tall son ahead of him while he chortled in pleasure.

"My little surprise," he bawled gleefully. "Got us a cook."

Christine felt her cheeks burn. The young man was more handsome than she had remembered. He studied her openly, his eyes indicating his own pleasure.

"You remember Miss Delancy?"

Mr. Kingsley had not ceased slapping his son on the back. Rather worse than the tapping pencil.

Boyd nodded. Christine noticed the twinkle in his eyes. "Who could forget?" he said with a courtly little bow and a smile at her.

"Who could forget? That's good. Who could forget?" Mr. Kingsley thumped his son's back again. "Well, I'll tell you one thing. You won't forget the chicken and dumplings. No siree."

"Excuse me," said Christine, flushed and

a bit uncertain. "I need to finish dishing up."

"May I help?"

Boyd's question surprised her. "No. No, thank you. I'll just . . . I'll . . ." She gave up and hurried from the room.

"Let's sit down," she heard Mr. Kingsley say. "She'll be right in."

Christine managed to get the rest of the food into serving bowls without spilling or dropping anything. After finally sitting down herself, she looked to Mr. Kingsley, wondering if he would offer a table grace. But he just said, "What are we waiting for? Let's eat!" as he grabbed up the nearest bowl.

It was a rather boisterous meal—though Christine had very little to contribute to the conversation. She wished she could have eaten in the kitchen as she had done before. She heard many lively stories about university life. Then she realized that few of the stories had anything to do with classes or studies. Mostly they were of sporting events and dorm pranks.

"So how are your courses coming?" Mr. Kingsley eventually asked. "Still think you're going to like law?"

"Didn't I tell you? I dropped that field."

Mr. Kingsley lifted his head. "No," he said. "I don't think you told me."

"Sorry. Guess I was just so involved . . ." But there didn't seem to be any true contrition in his tone.

"When did you make the switch?"

"First of the semester."

"And what did you switch to?"

"I don't know—yet. Still haven't decided. I think journalism might be interesting."

Mr. Kingsley nodded, his eyes questioning. But his voice was still even, interested, as he said, "Journalism?" He nodded. "Sounds good."

Boyd turned to Christine and complimented her on the dumplings.

Mr. Kingsley interrupted with, "The girl's a wonder in the kitchen."

"Sure beats those second-rate restaurants you usually take me to," joked Boyd.

Christine flushed again.

"Have you had any courses in journalism?" Mr. Kingsley picked up the previous conversation.

"Not yet. Didn't want to jump into it in the middle of a semester."

"But you were taking classes—right?"

"Oh . . . right. I finished up a couple of arts classes."

"Arts?"

"General. They will apply to almost

anything I decide to take."

"So you've only got a couple classes?"

"Well, I have another one from the first semester."

"I thought you took a full load your first semester."

"Well . . . yeah . . . I started out that way. Some of them were just . . . useless rubbish. I dropped a couple. Ended up with only one I could use."

Christine felt very uncomfortable. She wished she did not have to sit in on this exchange. Even so, the two seemed most amiable. No criticism on the part of the father. No apology or embarrassment on the part of the son.

"Takes a while to settle into university life," Boyd went on. "You sort of have to find your way."

Mr. Kingsley agreed, seeming quite willing to accept his son's word for it.

"Well—next year you'll know what to expect. More what you want. You can work it out then."

Boyd nodded and asked for the plate of chicken.

"Save plenty of room for dessert. I had Miss Delaney make your favorite. Chocolate cream pie. I got a whiff of it. You'll want more than one piece, I'm sure."

After the meal the men stretched out in front of the blazing fire in the drawing room, and Christine hurried off to clean up the kitchen. She had no objection to riding the city's electric streetcars, but she did not feel comfortable being out alone too late at night. Had she still been in the North she would not have given the late hour a second thought. Christine felt much safer in the North than in the unfamiliar city.

"Come. Come sit and visit," invited Mr. Kingsley, extending a hand to her when she stepped into the room to bid them a good-night.

"Oh . . . no. Thank you. I must get on home. I'm not even sure how late the trolley runs."

"Trolley? No trolley. No need. Boyd can take you in his car. Come and sit awhile."

Christine felt she had no choice in the matter. Reluctantly she laid aside her coat and went to join them. The younger man slid over on the couch and patted the seat beside him. With flushed cheeks, Christine accepted the invitation.

"So . . . has my father been treating you all right?" teased the young man. Mr. Kingsley laughed outright. Christine did not attempt an answer, feeling that none was really expected.

"I tried to get her to move in here," said Mr. Kingsley. "Room and board in exchange for a meal now and then."

Boyd looked at her closely, making her blush further. "Sounds like a good plan to me."

"Well, it didn't sound like a good plan to her. She turned me down."

Christine could feel two sets of eyes trained upon her. It made her most uncomfortable. "I just didn't think it would look right," she managed.

"Told her she could bring some other woman along," the father explained.

"I really have no . . . no other woman to bring," Christine defended herself.

"You could always bring Ol' Bones," Boyd put in.

At Christine's frown, he quickly amended the comment. "Whoops. Guess I should say Miss Stout."

Miss Stout? Ol' Bones? Christine was shocked at the young man's lack of respect, but his father only chuckled.

"I do not believe Miss Stout would be interested in making a move to accommodate me," Christine said, trying to keep her tone matter-of-fact.

Boyd smiled and shifted, stretching long legs across the heavy carpet. "Oh . . . I think Miss Stout would use any excuse available to be able to move in here," he said, raising an eyebrow somewhat cynically.

"I really must be going," Christine said as she stood to her feet.

Mr. Kingsley nodded. "Reckon the boy is a bit tired tonight too. He's had a long day of travel."

Soon the two were out in the cool night air, headed toward Boyd's automobile. Christine took a deep breath. It felt good to be fairly hidden in the darkness.

Boyd opened the car door and helped her into the vehicle.

"How many times a week do you favor us with a meal?" he asked as he started the engine.

"Oh no. This was a . . . a single event. Your father wanted to surprise you with a meal at home on your first night."

"I'm disappointed," he said, and he sounded sincere. "It was a delightful surprise, and I was hoping it would be repeated—regularly. You're quite sure we can't persuade you?"

Christine stammered for a reply. She couldn't find much to offer in the way of an argument. He was so gentlemanly. So confident and smooth. She felt like a backwoods bumpkin by comparison.

The car purred effortlessly along the empty streets. He asked, "What do you find to do in this cow town? What do you do for entertainment?"

"Entertainment?"

"Don't tell me my father doesn't leave you time for pleasure? Surely he doesn't work you all the time."

"Oh no. I have every evening free."

"And you. . . ?" he prompted.

"I read."

"Read?" The way he said the word made it sound like nothing could be more boring.

"I love to read," she said defensively.

"You know," he said with a laugh, "if you'll allow me, I guarantee I can find something for you that's a lot more exciting than that."

Christine did not answer.

They pulled up in front of her boarding-house, but before she could express her thanks and open her door, he reached over and took her hand. "How about it?" he pressed.

"I . . . I really must get in."

He had not let go of her hand, and she knew her heart was racing.

"You haven't answered my question."

"Well . . . it would . . . would depend," she said. "I wouldn't . . . I couldn't give a final answer. I've no idea what you might have in mind. I'd have to decide . . ."

His chuckle interrupted her words. "So it's not a straight-out no. That's a comfort." He gave her hand a squeeze. "Then I guess it's up to me to find something you'd agree to do. Right?"

She nodded, then realized it was too dark in the auto for him to see her. "Right," she managed.

He lifted her hand and gently kissed her fingers. "I accept the challenge."

Christine hurriedly withdrew her hand and scrambled from the car. She was visibly shaking as she made her way up the walk. She did hope she would meet no one in the hallway on the way to her room.

CHAPTER 8

Henry was sure his initial disbelief was showing on his face. He looked quickly again into the mirror, expecting to see her reflection revealing the same shocked recognition. Instead, he saw a perfectly poised barber going about the business of a haircut. There was nothing in her expression to indicate she remembered their earlier meeting.

Am I mistaken? Henry asked himself after another glance. *Surely not—unless she has a twin.*

Only the snip of the scissors interrupted the awkward silence. Now and then Henry lifted his eyes to the mirror. She efficiently worked on, her expression betraying nothing.

"You're the first barber I've ever had

that didn't talk my ear off," Henry said. He wanted to hear her voice again—make sure it was the one he remembered.

In the mirror he watched her shrug. "Sorry. I'm not given to small talk. Particularly on male topics. I'm not much for discussing hunting or fishing or ball games or motorcars."

He let the silence hold for a minute before he said, "Suppose you'll have to pick up on some of that stuff before too long with your son getting close to that age."

He thought he saw her shoulders stiffen and wondered if he had said the wrong thing. When she spoke again her voice was distant. "If you want a haircut—that I can do. If you want a chat, go to Jessie's Grill. Dozens of people in and out of there willing to spend the morning over coffee and gossip."

Yes, her voice did sound the same, even with its edge of coolness.

He felt he should apologize—yet he wasn't sure for what. So he said nothing. He certainly had not intended to pry. Or had he? *Yes,* he admitted silently. *I would gladly pry. I would like to ask her how she is doing. If she got over the death of her husband. If her little boy is missing a father. If she is making it on her own. Why she is cutting hair in a men's barbershop by the name of Sam's.*

Then with a quickened heartbeat he realized he would also like to know if she had ever married again.

But he asked none of those questions. Silently he watched her finish the last few snips. She did indeed give a great haircut. And sadly—to his way of thinking—it was also one of the fastest he had ever received. He waited for her to remove the cape and apply the little brush to the nape of his neck. He stood and reached in his pocket for money. He was so tempted to add a bit to the cost, but he checked himself. He had the feeling she would not understand nor accept what looked like a handout. He gave her the coins and their hands brushed ever so slightly. Something deep inside responded—as though he had some strange right, some connection to this woman. Hadn't he earned it . . . in a way?

But no. Certainly not. He had only done his duty as an officer of the law. He had held her . . . let her weep. Wiped her tears, even offered to brew her some tea, which she had promptly refused. But he had earned no rights. He had no claim on this attractive, vulnerable young woman whose face had been before him so many days on the trail. Had filled so many of his dreams out under the frozen stars. No claim at all.

And the little boy. Henry had held him as a baby. His mother had passed the infant to him while she went into the next room to get him a dry diaper. It was one of the few times in his life he had held a baby. In Indian villages, babies in most instances were in their cradleboards, tied securely to the back of a mother, older sister, or grandmother. Yet holding that little child—he remembered now that she had called him Danny—looking into his eyes and knowing he would never have his own memories of the father he had just lost, had affected Henry in a deep, unexplainable way. Even now he felt the strange longing to somehow reach out to this child. But how? He was sure any move he made would be totally misconstrued.

He placed his Stetson on his head and gave her a nod. "Good cut," he said, not daring to accompany the brief compliment with a smile.

"Thanks," she said simply, and she didn't smile either.

He had never seen her smile. Only weep. Oh, she had crooned words of love to her baby, but even then the tears were still falling down her cheeks. He longed to see her smile now—to know that things were all right in her world. But he turned without another word and left her little shop.

His two junior officers turned to look at him when he entered the small building that housed the RCMP office. Laray was the one who spoke first.

"See you got yourself a haircut."

Henry turned to place his Stetson on the shelf and rubbed his neatly clipped head. "Yup."

He took his seat at his desk and pulled some papers forward.

"So—what did you think of Sam?" Rogers pursued the interrogation.

Henry studied the form before him, though his brain was not making sense of any of the words. The two men had no idea what he was feeling inside. What intense emotions had been stirred by this chance meeting. Nor could he share his thoughts and emotions with them. He struggled to keep from showing the agitation that he felt. One hand reached up to run a finger along the line of his mustache.

She was not Sam. He knew that. He had done paper work at the time of her husband's accident. He knew her name well. It had been on his lips, whispered in his prayers, many times over the years. But he said nothing about the name. "She does a good job," he answered offhandedly.

Henry felt the exchanged glances. The fellows were expecting something more.

"Come on, Sarge," said Laray. "Every young buck for miles around gets his hair cut at least twice as often as he needs to. Including me." He laughed loudly.

"He's been trying for more than a haircut," put in Rogers. "So far he hasn't gotten to first base."

"She's as pretty as a picture—and as cold as an icehouse in the middle of a blizzard," Laray observed. His laughter had died now. Henry thought the young man likely wasn't used to getting the cold shoulder.

"Even the uniform doesn't turn her head," Rogers went on.

"I asked her out once—ever so politely—and got told straight off that her place was a place of business. Period. No social engagements were arranged there." Laray was mimicking her by the last sentence.

Henry felt himself scowling. Was that

what the young woman had to face in her shop? Offensive, heavy-handed flirts? No wonder she was distant and had no time for chatter.

He bit down on his tongue. He was so close to reprimanding the two men. Telling them to keep their hands off. To treat the young woman as she should be treated—as a lady.

"Next time I go, I'm gonna ask her for a shave too," said Laray, rubbing his hand up and down his cheek.

Henry could no longer hold his anger in check. "Look," he said, too sharply. "Treat her with respect—or stay out of her shop."

Both heads jerked in his direction. Henry could see questions in the two sets of eyes. Just male banter. Nothing harmful in that.

He eased back in his chair.

"She's . . . she's a citizen of the town . . . with rights," Henry went on more evenly now. "We don't want any complaints brought. Especially against the Force."

The two faces before him looked rather sober, and they both nodded. Rogers even flushed.

"I think she's plenty used to it," Laray said a bit defensively, but he was no longer cocky. "Fellows are talking all the time about how they tried this or said that."

"Well . . . I don't want that kind of talk coming from this office," Henry said, his words firm. As the one in charge he was expected to give orders. The two subordinates nodded, eyes on their desks.

"What I don't get," said Laray after some minutes, "is where wooing a gal stops and . . . and stepping over the line takes over."

Henry reached up and rubbed at his head, feeling once again the smoothness of the new haircut.

"Okay," he said, looking at Laray's expression of honest concern. "I admit it's a tough call . . . at times. Maybe I have to go back to what my mother taught me. She says you don't want to *mar*—to damage—a good relationship. So you think, MAR. Motive, approach, and response. MAR."

"Wha-at?" wailed Laray. "This sounds like . . . like school."

"What's your motive?" Henry continued, ignoring Laray's exaggerated sighs. "Are you just out to . . . to get your own pleasure, or do you have true respect for the other person?"

Laray seemed to be thinking about it.

"Okay," he said at length. "I follow."

"Approach," said Henry. "Have you gone about it in a proper, socially acceptable way?"

Again Laray nodded. Rogers was leaning on an elbow, listening.

"Response," Henry went on. "If your advances are—or appear to be—unwelcome, then back off."

"What about 'Faint heart never won fair lady'?" asked Rogers.

Henry reached into his wastebasket, crumpled up a sheet of paper, and hurled it toward Rogers. "Come on," he joked, "I'm not a psychologist. How do I know?" He stood and reached for his Stetson. "I'll ask my mother next time I see her." The three men laughed, and Henry said, "You've your orders—let's get busy."

A busy and troubling day followed that little exchange. A farm accident meant a trip to the city hospital with an injured farmer. A domestic dispute had to be settled in a ramshackle cabin on the edge of town. Two young boys set a fire out behind an old, unused livery barn. A woman was bitten by a dog that was feared to be rabid. A rancher reported that some of his stock was missing. By the end of the day there was little time for small talk as the three officers busied themselves with lengthy reports, stomachs grumbling in complaint. Even Jessie's food would be welcomed. And bed? Bed would look awfully good.

Henry was very glad when Sunday arrived. It had been a busy, tiring week and emotionally exhausting. The unexpected encounter with the young woman whom he had met under such difficult circumstances almost five years previously had churned up a whole lot of feelings and questions he thought he'd finally gotten under control. Now he found himself watching for her as he walked the streets of the small town. He could not keep from closely studying every group of children he saw in the playground or in yards of homes. But he had not spotted Danny again. Nor his mother. It seemed ironic to be so close—yet so unable to help them as he yearned to do.

He dressed for church wishing he'd purchased a civilian suit. After a shave he studied himself in the mirror. *She gives a good haircut,* he thought as he once again ran a hand over his hair. He backed away hurriedly, surprised at how near she was to his conscious thought.

Vigorously he applied blackening to his already shining boots. Then he dusted off his Stetson and set out for a quick breakfast at Jessie's. At least eggs were not spiced. He'd have eggs and toast and a cup of her strong coffee.

After being served, he still had plenty of time, so he lingered over a second cup of coffee, the talk and banter swirling, mostly unnoticed, about him. He had not been in town long enough to be considered one of them. Folks still had to get a feel for this new lawman. See if he had a human streak. So most of the conversation was not meant for him. He was lucky, at this point, to get an occasional nod and a good-morning.

After church he had no idea how he would spend the rest of the day. Church would take only a couple of hours. What he would do after that, he had no idea. He stared into his cup, and a feeling of intense loneliness suddenly engulfed him. He envied Rogers, who was bringing in his wife and young family in a few weeks, finally having found accommodation for them. No wonder Rogers was walking with a lighter step.

Henry's thoughts turned again to home. He hadn't fully appreciated as a kid just how fortunate—how blessed—he'd been. Oh, he remembered the enormous change between the two households. From the trouble, bickering, and often outright fighting of his earliest memories, he had suddenly come into a family where he was loved. Loved and nurtured. And even shown respect as an individual. There had been no doubt in his mind from that time on as to "what he would be when he grew up." He'd be a Mountie. Just like his father. He'd walk tall—and proud—and help people.

He looked down at the uniform. He was still proud to be a Mountie. Still wore the uniform with dignity. But inside the scarlet tunic beat a human heart. One that longed for intimacy—not aloofness. One that yearned for a relationship, rather than only duty. He sighed deeply. Maybe for him that would never be. Maybe he would be one of the men "married to the Force." He hoped not. His father and mother had been a living example of how good a marriage could be.

He put down his cup and stood. It was time to walk the short distance to the little church. He needed that time in worship this morning. Even though the church family still held back, in awe of his position and uniform, they welcomed him with kindly smiles. He felt a comfort in the familiar hymns, a contentment in the familiar words of Scripture. A completeness somehow. It managed to bring balm to his soul. To put his world back into proper perspective.

He felt his stride quicken. He was anxious to join with others in praise and worship.

The church was small and the pews were almost full when he entered and removed his hat. An usher welcomed him and pointed out a place. He walked in as unobtrusively as possible, but he sensed heads turning.

The service began, and he shared the hymnbook with the young lad beside him. The woman at the piano did a fine job of following the notes. His thoughts went to his mother. He had loved to watch her play. Had enjoyed the fluid motion of her slim hands just as much as he had enjoyed the music. It was always a marvel to him that fingers could move in such unison, yet individually, each seeking out the key that produced the note desired. He watched this woman's hands now with similar awe at their skill.

They sang three hymns in a row. By the end of the third his heart felt truly focused on God in worship. He had been lifted out of himself, his workaday world, his isolation. He felt part of the family of God.

The preacher was young. Though not yet a deep theologian, he had some thought-provoking insights to share. Challenges for the congregation as they faced another week. Henry was sorry to hear the last amen . . . now thrust back into the world to somehow fill in the hours of this long day.

He was on the wide front steps of the church before he saw the boy. The child was swinging on the handrail, chatting excitedly with a small group of youngsters. Henry was about to move forward and speak to the boy himself when he heard a voice almost at his elbow. "Danny, careful—you'll fall."

Danny scooted back onto the steps, but without a moment's hesitation in his report—something about neighborhood puppies, and there were six of them, and he sure would like to have one, and . . .

Henry did not dare turn around. He was

131

sure he would say or do something she wouldn't like. She might even be suspicious of his attendance in church.

A child ducked in front of him, and he was forced to halt midstep. He felt a brief nudge and heard a soft "Sorry."

He turned to reassure the person of no harm done and found himself looking directly into her violet eyes. He couldn't speak. Did not offer a smile. She was so close. Almost in his arms again.

"Sorry," she said again, her voice not more than a whisper. Her face was flushed, and she seemed as uncomfortable as he was. He managed to nod. That was all.

The brief encounter disturbed him. He didn't stop to change from his dress uniform. He didn't go back to Jessie's for some of her Sunday special. Instead, he found himself heading out the dusty track that led from the town. He'd walk. It had been some days since he'd had a good walk. It was one more thing he missed about the North. He wished he had a dog to accompany him. At least then he'd have some companionship. Maybe one of those puppies . . . He brushed the thought aside and set out briskly. Maybe with time and miles he'd be able to walk himself out of his doldrums.

CHAPTER 9

Christine still wasn't sure she was doing the right thing. Boyd had been home for three weeks. Three weeks of phone calls and rose bouquets. Three weeks of office flirtations and dinner invitations, which she more and more reluctantly turned down. And now, here she was, finally having consented to a Saturday picnic in the park with some of his friends. She admitted to herself that she found him immensely attractive. She acknowledged that she felt a bit smug over the envy of the other girls in the office. But she also recognized the fact that she was still uncomfortable with finally giving in and going out with him.

"Can't wait to show you off," he was saying, whipping the fast-moving automobile around a sharp turn, his eyes not on the road as much as on her face.

Christine managed a smile in spite of her fluttering heart. She wasn't sure how she would fit in with Boyd's crowd. She knew little about them, but she did know they were not drawn from the group of young people from her church.

He reached for her hand and steered down the road with one hand on the wheel. His speed had not slackened.

Christine gave a bit of a squeeze and pulled her hand back, hoping he would return to proper driving.

"You nervous?" he asked with an impish grin.

She nodded, but she couldn't help but laugh. He always managed to bring her out of herself.

"Don't be," he said. "I've told them all about you."

She wondered just what he had said. It didn't make her feel any more at ease.

She grabbed for a handhold when Boyd cut the car sharply to the left and swung in under a grove of poplar trees. Feeling a bit shaky on her feet, she stepped from the car. She could see no one else around.

"Where is everyone?" she asked as Boyd lifted out the picnic basket.

"Actually," he responded with another grin, "there isn't anybody else. I just used that story to get you to come with me. I wanted you all to myself."

Her hands went to her face and her knees went weak. He watched her reaction closely, then howled with mirth. He reached over to give her arm a playful punch.

"They'll be here, little Miss Proper. Trudie is always late. She holds up everyone else. But it's worth it. She's a barrel of laughs."

Boyd spread out the blanket, tucked the picnic basket up against the trunk of a tree, and held out his hand. "Come. Want to see the river?"

Christine allowed herself to be led down the bank. The river was a bit of a disappointment, not clear and sparkling like the streams of the North. Nor did it flow with the same energetic enthusiasm. Still, it was flowing water. She would like to have sat down on the bank and listened to its song.

Boyd kept walking. "So what do you think of my old man?" he asked.

Surprised at the question, she answered, "He's . . . he's been a fine boss." Beyond that she had given little thought to Mr. Kingsley.

"Ol' Bones's had her eye on him for years."

Christine was very uncomfortable with his disrespectful familiarity with a woman old enough to be his mother.

"I've never been much excited about the prospect of that sour old woman as a new mother," he went on as if he'd picked up on her thoughts.

"Miss Stout has been kind to me," said Christine with stubborn loyalty.

He turned and pulled her close—too close—and whispered in her ear, "Who wouldn't be kind to you?"

She pushed away as gently but as firmly as she could.

"Okay. Okay," he laughed. "I get the message. Promise I won't go too fast."

A car horn from above them signaled the rest had arrived, and Boyd grabbed her hand to help her back up to the top. "Guess Trudie finally got her hair fluffed and her nails painted," he laughed as they climbed the steep path.

Five young people, laughing raucously, were scrambling out of a crowded auto— three fellows and two young women. Christine wondered which one was Trudie. She had picked her out even before Boyd made the introduction. She had flaming red hair that swirled about her lightly freckled face. Christine was not accustomed to such dramatic makeup and found the effect theatrical. But she soon realized that Trudie was indeed always on stage. From the moment she arrived, she had the group roaring with laughter. Her words and manner were rather flamboyant and loud, but her friends seemed to greatly enjoy her humor.

A lanky youth with a wide grin and a shock of dark hair falling forward over his face seemed to be the redhead's escort. They were about as different as rain and snow to Christine's thinking. The boy rarely opened his mouth—except to cram it full of the contents of the various picnic baskets. She had never seen such a ravenous appetite, not even in her brother Henry when he was a teenager.

Christine was uncomfortable eating without first thanking the Lord for the food. She managed to bow her head for a quick prayer before beginning her own sandwich, but the chatter around her had not slackened, and she found it difficult to concentrate.

Even with everyone eating heartily, the talk and laughter still had not slowed down.

"What happened to Maude?" asked Boyd around a chicken drumstick.

"She has a toothache," answered the young man in the blue-striped shirt. Christine thought his name was Jared.

"Can you imagine that?" chirped Trudie, holding her jaw in mock sympathy. "A toothache keeping her home. I'd never let a little thing like a toothache keep me from a party."

"Speaking of a party—where are the drinks?" asked Stephen, a short fellow with eyeglasses.

Boyd leaped to his feet and proceeded to his car and opened the trunk. "Help yourself," he called, and everyone but Christine hurried over to do so.

"What do you want, Christine?" he called to her. "Beer or wine?"

"I . . . no, thank you," she stammered as several pairs of eyes turned to stare. She felt embarrassed—and terribly disappointed. She had thought Boyd would know she would not drink alcohol.

"Christine's father is a cop," explained Boyd with a laugh, and all five broke into hilarious laughter. Christine did not understand the joke.

"So what *will* you drink?" Boyd asked as

he threw himself back down on the blanket beside her.

"I'll . . . I'm fine," she was quick to say.

"Next time we'll bring some soda pop," said Trudie in an affected way that drew another laugh.

"Lemonade," someone else offered, and they laughed more loudly.

"Hey, you guys, lay off," warned Boyd, and the laughter subsided.

Christine couldn't help being thirsty. Had she been in the North, she would have gone to the stream for a refreshing drink. But the murky waters of the nearby river did not tempt her at all.

The afternoon dragged by. They really didn't do anything. Just lolled about on the blankets, talking and laughing and at times sounding a bit vulgar. A few times Boyd warned them off with a look or a word. They continued to drain the bottles, and the more they drank, the louder and coarser they became. Christine ached to go home.

A rain cloud finally brought her release. They grabbed picnic baskets, blankets, and belongings and rushed to the cars. Christine breathed a prayer of thanks.

"You didn't have too much fun today, did you?" Boyd asked seriously on the drive home. He was driving much more slowly, both hands on the wheel. The rain continued to fall, the modern miracle of an outer windshield wiper keeping their vision clear.

"I'm sorry," said Christine honestly. "I guess I just don't fit with your . . . with your friends."

He nodded as though agreeing.

Well, that's the end of that, thought Christine, feeling a strange combination of sadness and relief.

"I won't ask you to do it again," Boyd continued, and now he did take a hand off the steering wheel to reach out to her. "Come over here." He smiled. "Please."

She slowly slid across the seat. He lifted an arm around her shoulders and pulled her closer yet.

"Next time we'll do something on our own."

Christine could not hide her surprise.

"You name it," he went on.

She turned to him. "You mean it?"

" 'Course."

Suddenly the day seemed brighter again. He did not plan to stop asking her out. He wasn't asking her to join his crowd. She could scarcely believe it.

"So where will it be?" he asked.

"I'll have to think about it."

"Okay." His arm tightened. "I'll give you until we get home."

She laughed in delight. She could laugh now. She'd not been able to laugh at the crude jokes on the picnic blankets, but now she laughed out of sheer joy.

They were soon pulling up in front of Christine's boardinghouse. "You're sure you have to go?" he asked her soberly.

"I'm sure. I have some things I need to do before tomorrow."

His arm tightened. "Have you thought about it?"

"I have."

"And. . . ?" he prompted when she went no further.

"How . . . how long do I have to wait for this date?" she asked, surprised at herself.

"An hour or two. Maybe less if you coax me."

She laughed again. "In that case—what about tomorrow morning?"

"Tomorrow morning? That's better than I dared hope." His arm pulled her closer against his side. "So where do we get to go tomorrow morning?"

"To church," she answered without hesitation.

"Church?"

She could hear the shock in his tone. It brought her a deep disappointment.

"You don't have to—if you'd rather not," she was quick to amend.

To her surprise he reached out to encircle her in his arms. "No," he said, sounding as if he had recovered. "A promise is a promise. Just . . . fill me in. What am I to do . . . and when?"

———————

True to his word, Boyd picked Christine up for church promptly at 9:45 the next morning. She could tell it was all very new to him. Very strange. She could feel him watching her closely to see how he should participate in the service. She smiled at him often and tried to make him feel at ease.

After the service several people greeted him, and she introduced him to any of those whose names she knew. But she could tell he was anxious to get away from the small congregation. He was edging toward the car, and she allowed herself to be led away as soon as she could do so without being rude.

"Well," he said once he was behind the wheel. "That was a new experience."

"Thank you," said Christine. "For going with me, I mean."

He merely nodded.

"Have you really never been to church before?" she dared ask.

"Never."

"That's sad. You've missed so much."

He did not respond.

"Did your . . . your mother attend church?" Christine knew she might be getting too personal, but she wanted to know.

"I don't remember *Mother*." It was said too sharply.

"I'm sorry," she said again.

"Look," he said, angrily turning to her. "There's not a thing you have done—or can do—about my mother. No sorrys. They don't fix anything. So let's just not bring it up, okay?"

Christine was shocked by his obvious emotional trauma. She wanted to say sorry again but didn't dare. She just nodded.

The stormy interchange was over as quickly as it had come. He looked at her and smiled. Even reached out for her hand. "Where should we go for dinner?" he said as if nothing had happened.

There had been no arrangement made for dinner. Christine's landlady would be expecting her at the boardinghouse table.

"Mrs. Green is expecting . . ."

"Phooey on Mrs. Green," he said dismissively. "She won't even notice you're gone. Besides, all she cares about is getting the money. As long as she has full pay, she'll be glad she didn't have to feed you."

"You don't know Mrs. Green. She doesn't even serve anyone until all of us are at the table."

"A cuff on the side of the head to Mrs. Green. She sounds like a spoilsport to me."

She managed a light laugh. "Maybe next time."

When they got to her place, he pulled over to the curb. Before she could thank him or open her door, he reached out and held her arm. His other hand raked through his hair with spread fingers.

"Look, Christine," he said. "I don't want you to get the wrong idea. About today."

She swallowed nervously.

"I . . . I don't think I can handle going to your church again. It makes me feel creepy. All that singing and talking about a guy who's been dead for nearly two thousand years. That's really not where I'm at."

She could have protested. The "guy" he

talked about was not dead. He was alive. But all she did was nod her head. That painful little sadness tugged at her heart again. It hadn't worked. Their worlds were too far apart. She should have known. She gave one more nod and turned to go.

"But I do want to see you again," he stopped her.

Slowly she shook her head. "It wouldn't work. You know that. I . . . I don't fit in your world, and you don't fit in mine."

"But there must be a . . . a third world," he protested.

She stared at him. What did he mean?

"We can make one. Please. I won't ask you to go out with my friends—and you don't ask me to go to your church. We'll just go places we can both enjoy. Things we can share."

Though her head was warning her not to be taken in, her heart yearned to at least listen.

"Our own two-person picnic," he rushed on. "The beach. Drives in the country. Dinner. We'll find lots of things," he finished with enthusiasm.

"I don't think—"

"Please. Let's just try it, Christine. If you're still uncomfortable . . ."

He didn't finish the thought, but he was wearing down her reserve. Breaking down the wall she had been carefully trying to construct.

"I'll . . . think about it."

He leaned across and kissed her cheek—ever so lightly. "And I won't think of anything else," he murmured against her hair before he straightened up.

She stood on the sidewalk and watched him drive away. She was in turmoil. She did want to go out with him again. In fact, she knew in her heart of hearts that she would agree. Yet there was an inner conflict that would not let her agree in peace.

CHAPTER 10

Though the detachment was kept busy, Henry felt the summer was slowly crawling by and time was standing still.

He had been in the area long enough to establish some first-name acquaintances. Not anything that could yet be called a true friendship, but at least townspeople who no longer seemed to hold their breath when he appeared on the scene.

Most of those were people from the church. The pastor in particular was warm and open with Henry. He appreciated having someone who shared his faith to join him for an occasional cup of Jessie's coffee.

But things had not changed with the young woman and her son. He still went for the periodic haircuts and was always politely received. But in spite of the fact they attended the same church, she remained distant and unresponsive.

He had noticed that she seemed like an entirely different person at church than in her shop—warm and outgoing, with a wonderfully warm smile and a delightful sense of humor. She doted on her son, but he guessed that was to be expected. Gradually he learned a few things just by keeping his eyes and ears open. Her mother also attended the church. She was a tiny lady with a big smile and hugs for everyone. She was the first person Henry knew whom he would have described as *bustling*. He noticed too that Mrs. Martin always seemed to have some package in her hand. A jar of fresh jam for some elderly couple, crocheted booties for the expectant mother, a fresh loaf of bread for a bachelor farmer. Everywhere the woman went she drew her little rainbow of happiness along with her.

Henry was not too surprised when she approached him one morning following the service. "I feel like I've neglected you," she apologized. "Is it too late to invite you for dinner? I never know which Sunday you are on or off duty, so I'm afraid I haven't been successful in planning ahead."

He smiled and thanked her. Yes, Sunday

dinner sounded wonderful, he quickly told her.

"I'm going to hurry on home," she continued. "You come whenever you're ready. It's that house on the corner of Fifth and Seventh. With the white picket fence. You can't miss it."

He thanked her and turned to finish his conversation with a rancher who was having problems with a marauding bear.

"I've lost a few healthy calves," the rancher continued as Mrs. Martin bustled away. "I think this here fella might be the cause. I've seen him a couple times and run across his spore several more. He's a big one—but lanky lookin'. Like maybe he hasn't been fattenin' up like he should. Gettin' closer to fall he's gonna get more and more desperate. Knows he needs that fat to get him through the winter."

Henry nodded, but in truth his mind had been on other things—about the possibility of learning more about "Sam" and her son. Surely, like all mothers, Mrs. Martin wouldn't mind discussing her daughter.

"I'll have one of the fellows look into it," he heard himself saying to the rancher. "Drop by the office and give us some details of the location."

The man thanked him, replaced his wide-brimmed hat, and ambled off in the direction of his horse.

Not wanting to rush the woman, Henry took his time walking to the house with the picket fence. When he arrived, the little lady met him at the door and led him into the living room. To his surprise, a man was sitting in the corner in an overstuffed chair, Bible in hand.

He smiled broadly, and before the woman could speak, he did. "Excuse me for not getting up. Got an awful mess of arthritis in my right knee." He extended a hand, and Henry could see that he also had a mess of arthritis in that. Henry was careful to shake with caution.

"My husband, Sam." The woman made the introductions and indicated a nearby chair. "You can just sit and get to know one another while I put on the meal."

Henry took the seat.

"Ma's been telling me about you," began the man named Sam. "Awful nice that you been joinin' the folks at church. Used to be able to go myself until this here arthritis laid me up."

"I'm sorry about that," Henry said sincerely. "Been giving you trouble for quite some time?"

"About two years now. Oh, it troubled me before that, but only in the last two years has it kept me in." He held out his right hand and studied it. "I got so I couldn't hold the scissors nor cut properly. Was afraid I'd cut off someone's ear." He chuckled. "That's when I talked my daughter into getting some training and taking over the shop. She needed something anyway." He stopped and waved the crippled hand. "But don't need to bother you with all that. Of no interest to you."

Oh, if he only knew, thought Henry, leaning forward in the chair. "No—please—go on," he said, trying to keep his tone casual. When the man looked at him curiously, Henry said, "I've . . . I've met your daughter. At the shop and . . . and at church," he quickly added, hoping that would make his interest seem unremarkable.

"Well, she's rather a private person. Don't know she'd like me going on about her personal matters." Sam closed down the conversation.

But all was not lost. Henry noted several pictures about the room. They showed the young woman from early childhood through her teen years. One in particular held his attention. It was the wedding picture, the beautiful bride and the young Swedish logger. Something twisted deep within him as he looked at their happy faces. What a tragic ending to such a beautiful beginning.

The last picture was of the woman and Danny. Henry could see it had been taken quite recently. Danny was probably about to celebrate his fifth birthday. Henry had to pull his eyes from the photo and try hard to concentrate on what Sam was saying.

". . . so my wife, she says, 'God has taken care of us all these years. He's not going to let us down now.' And then she went out and got herself a job at the grocer's. So between God and Martha"—he stopped to chuckle—"we're makin' out just fine. Then my daughter—she's buying Sam's. Pays a little each month. Doin' real good, though. Guess she must be a better barber than I was. Business has sure been boomin'."

So that's why little Danny spends his days in the care of Mrs. Crane, thought Henry. He'd wondered why the grandmother was not looking after the boy.

"One thing I feel bad about," the man went on, "is little Danny. Poor little fella lost his pa, and now he's got a crippled-up grandpa who can't do things with him. I'd looked forward to takin' him fishin', teachin' him how to throw a ball—all those things. And now these ol' hands and this here knee won't let me do anything like that."

"I've got some free time," offered Henry carefully, his throat tight. "I'd be glad to spend some with the boy." He tried to check his eagerness. "If his mother is comfortable with it, of course."

"She's pretty protective," Sam said, shaking his head.

"One can't fault her for that."

The fragrances coming from the kitchen were making Henry hope they soon would be called to the table. He hadn't realized how hungry he was—nor how anxious he was to taste real food, apologies to Jessie. He watched as the man opposite him reached down to rub his afflicted knee. Henry wondered if he was even conscious of doing so.

"You know," Henry dared say, "I spent much of my growing-up years in the North among the Indian people. They do wonderful things with their roots and herbs. Hardly ever see an Indian with arthritis. They have this bitter root they grind up and make into tea. Would you be interested in trying some if I could get it down here for you?"

Sam's eyes brightened with interest. "If they drink it and it doesn't kill 'em—guess it wouldn't kill me either." He chuckled.

"I'll talk to my father. He's back in Athabasca. But he often has contact with people who are in and out of Indian country. He might be able to get hold of some."

"What's your father do?"

"He's with the RCMP."

"That why you joined the Force?"

Henry nodded.

"Nice to have a son follow in your footsteps. I had hoped my boy . . ." He stopped.

"You have a son?"

"*Had* a son," he corrected. "Lost him in the Great War. Somewhere in Italy."

"I'm sorry," said Henry, genuine concern in his heart.

The man looked about the room. "Martha took down all his pictures. Moved them to our bedroom. Said she wanted to see him first thing every morning and last thing every night. His death was pretty hard on Martha. Hard on both of us."

Henry heard a movement in the doorway, and Mrs. Martin was there, her signature smile in place. *To look at her you'd think she's never had a sorrow in her life,* thought Henry.

154

"Here you go, Sam," she said, offering an arm. "Let me help you up. Here's your cane. Just take it easy, now."

They moved into the dining room where steaming dishes of food awaited them. There were even fresh-baked baking powder biscuits, and Henry's stomach growled in anticipation.

The meal was even better than it had smelled. Henry was embarrassed for being talked into seconds, but Mrs. Martin seemed pleased he was enjoying her meal.

"A hearty appetite is the nicest compliment to a cook," she assured him.

Henry found it very pleasant to just sit and chat about ordinary daily happenings and people of the community. It was such a nice change from filing reports about community mishaps and worse.

Mrs. Martin served the pie and refilled coffee cups. She settled into her chair and turned to Henry.

"Now, why don't you tell us a bit about yourself," she encouraged. "How long have you been a Mountie?"

"More than five years now," answered Henry.

"His dad was an RCMP officer," put in Mr. Martin.

"Really. So you grew up with the police."
Henry nodded.

"Where was your dad posted?"

"Mostly the North."

"You grew up in the North?"

"He says the Indians have some root medicine that he thinks might help my arthritis," noted Mr. Martin.

"Really?" Her eyes widened in interest. "I've heard of their herbs. Our daughter and her husband spent some time in the North."

Henry supposed he was to respond with question or comment, but he did not know what to say, so he said only, "That's interesting."

"She liked it there—at first. . . ." The woman's words trailed off sadly.

"Danny was born up there at Peace River," Mr. Martin explained.

"He doesn't remember anything about it—but he pretends he does," Mrs. Martin laughed. "He talks about 'my North' like he has some claim to it. He's always asking his mother, 'When are we going back to my North?' It's quite cute."

Henry forced a smile.

"Does your daughter plan to go back?" he finally asked, hoping his voice was even and casual.

156

"No . . . I don't think so. Not now. I think . . ." But Mrs. Martin again did not finish.

"There's nothing there for her now," Mr. Martin was quick to fill in. "Barbers aren't in too much demand along the trap-lines or in the logging camps," he joked to lighten the atmosphere.

They were just finishing their pie when the back door banged open and Danny skipped into the dining room. He ran straight to his grandfather. "Hi! How you feelin' today, Papa Sam?"

Mr. Martin reached out with gnarled fingers and drew the boy close to his side. He kissed the tousled head before he re-plied. "I'm good . . . now."

"We came to see you."

"I see you did. You check with Granny. She might have another piece or two of that pie."

There was a quiet step behind him, and Henry knew without turning around that the boy's mother had arrived in the room. He could almost sense her moment of hesi-tation. Then she moved forward.

"How are you, Papa?" she asked as she proceeded toward the man. She bent to place a kiss on his forehead.

Mrs. Martin had sprung up from her chair. "There's a seat for you, dear. Pull out that chair for Danny. I'll get pie and more coffee."

"Mama—we've already eaten."

"Well, Danny can always make room for pie," she answered with a grandmother's certainty.

"Just a small piece, then."

"You've met Sergeant Delaney?" Sam Martin asked.

Henry stood to his feet to acknowledge the introduction. He nodded silently, wondering if he should extend his hand or wait for her to make the move.

She just nodded. "Hello" was all she said. Then as an afterthought she waved her hand toward the table. "Please . . . finish your pie."

Henry took his seat again.

Danny had rushed off to the kitchen to supervise his grandmother's serving up of the pie. Henry could hear them.

"Who's that man?"

"He's our guest."

"He's got a red coat. Does that make him a Mountie?"

"Yes. He's a policeman."

"Tommy says policemans are to lock you away in big iron cages."

"Tommy is wrong. We'll talk about it later."

Mr. Martin turned to his daughter with a question, probably to cover up the kitchen conversation.

"How has your week gone?"

She nodded. "It's gone." Then she smiled and added, "Fairly good, actually."

"Sergeant Delaney here has just been telling us about the North. He was raised up there. Also worked up there. Says there may be a chance the Indians would have some tea that would help my arthritis."

But Henry wondered if the young woman had been following her father's comments. He felt her eyes upon him, studying his face. "Really?" he heard her say.

Mrs. Martin and Danny returned, Danny carrying his own piece of pie. Mrs. Martin had another for her daughter and a cup of coffee in the other hand.

"Really, Mother. I couldn't eat anything. Just the coffee. Thank you. Danny—my goodness. That piece is awfully large."

"It's my favorite," explained Danny, forking in his first bite.

"Favorite or not, you're going to have a tummy ache."

"No, Mama, I won't. Gramma's pies

159

don't give tummy aches."

A chuckle rippled around the table. Only Danny missed the joke. He was much too busy enjoying his pie.

"I'm sorry to have barged in," his mother said. "I had no idea you had a guest. I thought you'd be all done with your dinner."

"We've just been chatting over our dessert," said her mother.

"As soon as Danny eats his pie we'll be off and leave you to finish your visit."

Henry was quick to offer his first comment since her arrival. "Please, don't feel you need to go. I was just about to take my leave. I've so enjoyed the dinner and the visit I'm afraid I've stayed much longer than I intended."

Mr. Martin turned to his daughter. "Sergeant Delaney has kindly offered to—" He broke off. "I guess we should talk about it sometime when we are alone." He nodded toward the young boy. "Best not get any hopes up before we get it sorted out," he added in an undertone.

Henry already felt certain what her answer would be. He cast a quick glance at her face, and he didn't think she had changed her mind.

"I've done a fair bit of outdoor activity

with young boys," Henry said in an effort to reassure her. "Camping. Fishing. Snowshoeing. Mushing. Young boys love the out-of-doors. I thought it might be one way I could help out at the church. Work with the boys. My father—that was how he first talked me into attending his Sunday school class." Seeing their expressions of curiosity, he hurried on. "I was adopted. My RCMP father taught the boys' class in Athabasca when I was a kid. I don't suppose I would have ever been interested in church if it wasn't for him."

Henry was touched by her parents' evident warmth and interest, but she said, "That's a great idea," without much enthusiasm. "For older boys."

Henry nodded and rose to go. It was difficult to express his heartfelt thanks to his host and hostess because of the keen disappointment he felt. It was clear that the younger woman was not going to open any doors to friendship.

CHAPTER 11

Boyd did find interesting things for them to do. Reluctantly at first, Christine agreed to outings. First a drive in the country. Then a picnic along the river. Then a concert. Out to dinner. Soon it was expected that they'd date each weekend. Christine had done a lot of praying about the matter to begin with, but gradually she pushed her concerns aside and began to count the days, living for that weekend event with Boyd. Then it became twice a week. Three times.

There was no mention of church, though Christine continued to pray that Boyd would change his attitude concerning God. Occasionally there was a casual mention of his friends. "My friends are having a party. Want to go?" Or "They're meeting at the beach this Saturday. Interested?" Christine always shook her head. She had no desire to try to fit in with that crowd. "You go if you like," she would say.

Sometimes he would sulk, turning cold and angry. Her heart sank when he was in that mood. But always, by the end of their date, he changed back to the attentive suitor she appreciated. Most of the time they did indeed have delightful times together.

She had no idea what he did with his days when he was home from college for the summer. She knew he did not have a job. From snippets of conversation, she understood that he was not an early riser. His father joked about him at times but always in good humor. "Boyd's resting up for university life," or "Boyd's a growing boy. Needs his sleep."

He did spend time tinkering with his car. In fact, he now had two cars. Why, Christine could not imagine, but he did enjoy the hours with wrenches and grease. "I think Boyd could make anything run," Mr. Kingsley boasted proudly. "Listen to that baby purr. Soft as a kitten."

Christine would smile. She was willing to accept the purring motor as an outstanding accomplishment.

But all through the glorious yet troubling months of their short summer, Christine continued to feel an uncomfortable sense that something was not quite right. She was getting too involved. The changes being made were not for the good. Instead of Boyd being more open to her faith, he seemed to be coaxing her more and more into his world. She had resisted—had told herself she was being firm. Strong. But was she? She prayed harder. "God, change him" was the heart of her prayers. Already she knew she did not want to lose him.

With the end of summer approaching, Christine knew Boyd was again leaving for college. "Why can't you transfer here?" she asked as he drove her home after their last dinner together. She recognized her own voice as pleading.

"I've started out in Toronto. I want to finish there."

Christine did not say that, from what she had gathered, he had not had too auspicious a start.

"I'll be home for Christmas," he said cheerfully. "That's only a few months."

Christine was sure they would be very long months. She had unwisely lost touch with the church group her age. Her attendance at the Sunday morning service had not stopped, but that was as far as her commitment now would go.

He pulled the car in against the curb and put it in neutral. "I'll miss you," he said, and his voice was warm and genuine. He pulled her close and kissed her. She knew she would miss him too. With all her heart.

She wanted to tell him she would be praying for him, but she swallowed the words along with the tears in the back of her throat.

"You'll write?" she asked as she clung to him.

He laughed. "I'm not much good at writing. I'll phone."

Christine thought of the common phone in the hall at the boardinghouse. She knew that under the circumstances the calls would not be very satisfactory.

"I can only use the phone for five minutes at a time," she informed him sadly. "And then for one call a night."

"Hey," he said suddenly, "why don't you take my dad up on his offer? Move in. No reason you should still be sitting over here dictated to by that Mrs. Whatever-her-color-is."

Christine laughed in spite of her aching heart. "Mrs. Green."

"I've never cared much for your Mrs. Green," he continued. "She's a pompous little dictator."

"You don't even know Mrs. Green."

"I've run into her a few times when I've come to get you. She's always sharp and sour and looks at me like I came to steal the silver. Worse than Ol' Bones."

"She's not. She's been most kind to me." She pulled away slightly. He tightened his arm around her shoulders. "Let's not fuss," he whispered against her hair. "This is our last night together."

She didn't need to be reminded.

"Well . . . why not?" he asked again, nuzzling her hair.

"I . . . don't know. It just doesn't—"

"Is it the cooking? Hey—if you don't want to cook, don't cook. Just live there. Be good for the old guy to have some company. And he likes you. Lots."

"It's not the cooking. I like to cook. It's just . . . well, it doesn't seem proper for a girl to be living . . . like that."

"Proper to whom? Why should you care what others think? If you were at the house, I could call you anytime I wanted and talk for as long as I cared."

It was tempting.

"Come on," he coaxed further. "Just think—when I come home for Christmas, you would be there waiting for me."

She would like that. She'd really like that. "I'll . . . I'll think about it." She swallowed hard. Even thinking about it was against her better judgment. Well . . . she'd pray about it. That was safe enough. Dared she say that to him?

She stirred. "Mrs. Green locks the door at nine."

"See what I mean? She's a tyrant. You can't even live your own life. Move in with Dad."

"I have to go. Really."

"Not yet."

"But I must. I don't want to be locked out."

"I'll take you home with me. Now. We'll get your things and tell Mrs. Green to stick the key in her ear and you're out of here."

"No—please. Not tonight. I . . . need some time to think about this. To pray . . ."

"I thought you were getting over that praying stuff." He was angry now. She hadn't wanted him to be angry—hadn't wanted their last evening together to end like this. She wished to turn her face against his shoulder and cry, knowing instinctively that he would hold her close and comfort her. But there was no time for comfort. At any minute Mrs. Green would be heading for the door, key in hand. Christine put a hand up to his lips. "Please," she whispered, "I need to go."

He not only released her, he almost pushed her away. He was already reaching for the gearshift before she could even open the car door.

She reached the door just as Mrs. Green came down the hall, jingling the keys in her hand. Christine managed a smile and a "good night," but it required every ounce of will she had. She wanted to do nothing other than throw herself on her bed and weep. Boyd was leaving in the morning, and they had parted with a quarrel.

When Christine dragged herself into the office the next morning, a lovely bouquet of red roses graced her desk. The card said simply, *Love, Boyd*. She wondered if he had ordered the flowers before or after his angry departure. She pushed that thought aside and buried her face in the blooms, drinking deeply of the fragrance. Tears threatened to come again, but she willed them away.

"Mr. Kingsley wishes to see you," said Miss Stout once again.

Christine pulled herself away from the flowers and turned toward the massive door leading to the office. She dreaded the coming exchange. Had Boyd told his father they had parted company with words? Had he declared they were through?

She braced herself with a deep breath and entered. The familiar head came up. A big grin welcomed her.

"Well . . ." he said, leaning back as though he expected the visit to take a while. "Got Boyd off to school this morning."

He nodded to the chair before his desk, and Christine sat down. She began to wonder what this was all about. Surely he didn't call her into his office just to tell her what she already knew.

"You've been good for my boy." His statement surprised her. "Steadied him down. He's not as flighty as he used to be. I appreciate that," he continued, obviously fighting to keep his voice controlled. His unusual show of emotion made Christine wish to weep.

"He was talking to me this morning before he drove out. Says he's really going to miss you."

Christine's heart sang. He wasn't still mad at her.

"Boyd thinks," he went on, "that it would be so much better for you—for the both of us—if you'd just move on over to the house."

So that was it. Boyd was having his father put on some pressure.

"No use your paying room and board and sitting over there all by yourself. Besides, then he'd be able to call you more. Keep in touch. I suppose he gets a bit lonely down at that university. Only natural. He's not good at letters. But then, neither am I. We use the phone."

Christine said nothing. Her momentary relief that Boyd still cared for her had now turned into another disappointment.

"It would mean a lot to me to have you keep contact with him," Mr. Kingsley was saying. "I'm not hiding that any. I'm afraid he gets a little . . . well . . . they can be a bit wild on those university campuses. Drink too much. Party too much. Only natural. Wild oats and all. But if he had you to call and chat with every night . . . then he'd pay a bit more attention to the studies."

So I'm to be your son's policeman, Christine's thoughts clamored, *keeping him in line via the telephone wires.* She began to shake her head, her heart heavy.

"Now—don't go saying no until you've thought about it. Nothing wrong with the plan that I can see."

"I told Boyd I'd pray about it," she finally said, hoping it would close the conversation and let her escape further argument.

"He said that."

Christine had the feeling that, like his son, Mr. Kingsley thought praying was a total waste of time and only delayed a decision.

"Don't take too long," he said. "We should be making our plans. Boyd will want to know."

Christine nodded and rose to her feet. She did hope she was dismissed. The conversation had made her extremely uncomfortable. Mr. Kingsley moved his chair forward again, and Christine knew the conversation was over. She moved quickly to the door.

She was opening the door when he called, "Roses okay?"

She stopped and looked back, sorting

through his words and his meaning. "They're beautiful."

"Boyd had me get the florist out of bed this morning, get him on down to the shop, and have them ready. Wanted to be sure you had them first thing."

"They're beautiful," Christine said again and quietly closed the door.

Christine did not move in with Mr. Kingsley. She did pray about it, but she knew even as she had said the words that prayer was not necessary. She knew deep within herself it was not the right thing to do. One way she knew was when she imagined herself trying to explain the arrangement to her parents.

Mr. Kingsley was not happy with her decision—nor was Boyd. But she started their months apart by writing every day. Just because Boyd was not good about letters did not mean she couldn't be. He did call. Two or three times a week to begin with. This meant Christine called home fewer times. She did not want to use up her precious allotted time in conversations with her folks. She missed that. But it seemed a small price to pay. Her parents would be with her always.

But then the telephone calls from the university came less and less frequently. Boyd told her the classes were keeping him busy—and Christine hoped that it was so. He had decided that journalism wasn't for him after all, and he was now taking some sociology courses.

Christine, who usually enjoyed the first snowfall, walked home with drooping shoulders. It was just something cold and messy and not at all welcomed. But at least the months were passing. Snow meant it would be time for Christmas soon. Her folks were expecting her home for Christmas. She had thought about how much fun it would be to take Boyd with her. Show him what a real family Christmas was all about. But that would leave Mr. Kingsley all alone. She couldn't do that. She gave up the idea.

Her letters soon slacked off to twice a week. Then once a week. There really was nothing much to say, and with Boyd not responding in kind, there was nothing to refer to on his end of things. She really knew very little about his university life. When they talked on the phone, they were hurried. He asked about her day and her plans and told her he missed her and hoped she was fine. It didn't take long at all to use up five minutes.

Occasionally there were disagreements. Boyd still did not understand what he called her stubbornness in refusing to move in with his father. He still was upset if he called on Sunday and was told she was at church. Christine felt he should know that's where she would be; then she reminded herself of the time change. Perhaps Boyd had forgotten to factor it in.

Christine decided that long-range courtships were not very satisfying. *Courtship?* Was that where she really was? If so, she needed to do some serious sorting and thinking. Boyd still had not made any move whatsoever toward her faith. Could she seriously consider him as a potential life partner? She'd pray harder.

CHAPTER 12

Elizabeth found herself pacing the floor as she anxiously waited for Wynn to come home. He was not later than usual, and normally she kept her emotions firmly in control. But her latest phone conversation with Christine had left her agitated. Even Teeko whined and shifted positions in the room at her restlessness. She heard the dog but paid little attention.

Elizabeth heard Wynn let himself in the door. She and Teeko both were facing him as he entered the room. His eyes moved from the face of his wife to the whining dog.

"Something wrong with him?" he asked as he removed his coat.

Elizabeth looked quickly at the husky. "I don't think so. Why?"

"He doesn't normally just lie there and

let me walk in. Teeko meets me at the door and nearly bowls me over."

At the sound of his name, Teeko leaped to his feet and went bounding forward, tail sweeping great arcs from side to side. He appeared to be fine. Wynn reached over to take the silky head between his palms and rock him back and forth. The dog rumbled his pleasure.

"Supper's ready," said Elizabeth, pulling her thoughts back together. She started for the small kitchen where the evening meal had been prepared.

"Be there just as soon as I get some grime off my hands," Wynn responded and disappeared into the bathroom.

He came back out refastening his cuff buttons. "Whew," he said. "Wish it was as easy to wash away the mental grime."

"Mental grime?" Elizabeth was putting out the bowl of mashed potatoes and the small platter of venison steaks. She went back for the carrots as Wynn continued his comments.

"Some days one has no choice but to deal with society's filth."

"And this was one of those days?" she asked over her shoulder.

He nodded. "Our world isn't getting any

better—or cleaner, Elizabeth. I don't know how people can treat one another the way they do. Or themselves, for that matter."

She did not ask questions. She wasn't sure she wanted to hear the answers. "I talked to Chrissie," she said instead. She saw she had his immediate attention.

"How are things?"

"I gather she is still very involved with that young man—though she didn't say so directly."

"I thought he was away at university."

"Oh, he is. But they correspond. Well . . . she corresponds. He phones. She is always antsy when I call since he might be trying to get the line. She quite cut me off today. She did apologize but said he hadn't called yet this week, and she was sure he'd try tonight."

He took his usual place at the table. "Is that what upset you?" he asked quietly.

"I didn't say I was upset."

He smiled. "No . . . and if you're honest, I don't think you'll say that you're not."

"Well, maybe I'm upset—a little," she admitted, "but I don't think it was that. At least . . . at least not only that."

She looked at her husband waiting patiently for her to continue. "I don't know. I can't really put my finger on it. She just seems . . . different. Distant. She's rather evasive and sometimes almost testy. It's . . . it's just not like Christine," she finished lamely.

"Wish we could get that fella up here and take a look at him," muttered Wynn as Elizabeth joined him at the table. "I've a feeling that would answer a lot of our questions."

"Well, having her home for Christmas will help. At least we'll be better able to figure out where she is—what's going on with her. Thankfully it's only a few weeks away."

"What about Henry? Has he worked out his duty roster?"

"I still haven't heard. He was having a hard time trying to schedule each of the officers a bit of time off. It's difficult when you have so few men. But of course you know all about that. I remember some Christmases when you had to go out . . ." Elizabeth shook her head and didn't finish.

"I expect he'll end up staying there," Wynn said slowly. "One of his men is married. He'll need time with his family. The other young officer won't be able to take all the shifts alone. Unfortunately, Christmas can be a tense time. Lots of people celebrate too much."

"Not *too much*—just in the wrong way," corrected Elizabeth soberly.

They now joined hands, and Wynn led them in the evening table grace. Elizabeth passed the meat platter, a sigh escaping her lips. "You know . . . it used to be so easy when they were little and all we had to worry about was keeping them fed and clothed and happy."

"You worry too much."

"I've told myself that dozens of times."

The dog yawned and stretched out beside Wynn's chair.

"It's . . . it's just that they are so far away. I feel like I've lost contact."

"Do you think it would be easier if they were close and you were more involved?"

"I honestly don't know. All I know is that I feel . . . disconnected, and it's frightening."

His smile was sympathetic. "You've raised them well, Elizabeth. You have a God you can trust."

"I know. I shouldn't worry."

"What exactly did Christine say?" Wynn asked when he pushed back his empty plate.

Elizabeth moved to get the tea. "Not too much. It was more what she *didn't* say. Mr. Kingsley and his son have both put pressure on her to move into the Kingsley house—"

"She's not considering that, is she?" She heard genuine concern in his voice.

"She told them no—again. But I'm afraid if they keep at her about it, she might give in. I'd hate to see her do that. I think it would be a dreadful mistake."

He nodded in agreement. "Maybe I should give her a call."

"Maybe you should call that Kingsley fellow."

"I'd rather not," his answer came quickly. "Christine might see it as interference. Like we don't trust her."

"Do we?" She studied his face as she continued. "Oh, I know we trust Christine. She's stood firmly for what she knows is right. But if they keep on badgering her—pushing her—what young girl on her own can stand against that? Particularly when one of them is her boss and the other seems to be capturing her heart. She said that Mr. Kingsley thinks she's a good influence on his son. Now, I ask you—why does his son need a good influence? What kind of young man is he? Christine won't say much. Just that she's sure we'd like him. Then she goes on about the beautiful roses he sent or the dinner at the fancy restaurant. As though that makes a man. I just don't like the sound of the whole thing."

"He's going to be home for Christmas?"

Elizabeth nodded. She could feel the worried frown on her forehead, and she consciously made an effort to relax her expression.

"I'll talk to her." Wynn's confident tone was comforting.

"She told me she was cooking a supper for the boss tonight. She does that now and then. I think she might be trying to appease him for refusing his invitation to move to his house. She said he's having another couple in tonight as guests. His brother and his wife—I think. They are visiting the city."

"That shouldn't make her too late. I'll phone and leave a message for her to call when she gets back."

"She's already had her one call for today. From me. The landlady allows each boarder only one call a day."

"Even if we call her?"

"Well, if she talks to someone who calls in, then she can't make a call out, is the way I understand it."

181

"Boy, that's pretty rigid. I suppose they need rules. Some boarders would be on the phone all the time. Well, I'm going to give it a try anyway. Mrs. Green, is it?"

Elizabeth nodded, but she felt so frustrated with this feeling of being cut off from her children.

———

It was well after nine when the return call came from Christine. She sounded nervous. "Is something wrong?" was her first question to Wynn.

"Wrong? No, I just wanted—"

"Oh, thank the Lord," she exclaimed. "I was afraid something had happened. Especially since I already talked with Mother earlier."

"I'm sorry. I certainly didn't mean to frighten you. And I really didn't expect you to call back tonight. Your mother said you'd already had your call for today."

"I thought it might be an emergency, so Mrs. Green—"

"I'm sorry," Wynn said again.

"It's just . . . you never call twice . . . in one day."

"I didn't get to talk with you earlier when your mother did. I thought it was my turn." Wynn decided to change the subject. "Your mother said you were playing chef again. How did it go?"

"Fine," answered Christine, but her voice still sounded shaky.

He was truly sorry for giving her such a start. He quickly realized this call probably would do little to alleviate their concerns. She was far too emotionally wrought to express her other feelings.

"Tell me about it."

"I only have five minutes."

"You're right. Don't bother telling me about the meal. Tell me about you. How's everything going?"

"Fine."

"You still like your job?"

"Most days."

"And other days?"

"It gets a little hectic at times. Especially at month's end when everyone wants everything—right now. Then we get behind in the filing, and some get a little testy as we try to catch up."

"I wish I had someone to do my filing," he chuckled.

"Dad, you have no idea what filing is," she exclaimed. "With eight typists constantly spewing out sheaves of paper, it can bury a desk in a day."

He laughed outright. She was sounding much more like herself.

"Do you have to do it all?"

"No, we each do our own."

"Then why the fuss?"

"Everybody wants the file drawers at the same time. We practically push for them. It's like . . . it's like a bunch of moose at a wallow."

He laughed again.

She doesn't sound so bad, he was mentally assessing. *I think her mother is overly concerned.*

"So how's the young man?"

"You mean Boyd?"

"Yes . . . Boyd."

"Fine."

Now her voice had taken a different tone.

"Mother said you were waiting to hear from him. Did he call?"

"We called him from Mr. Kingsley's."

"And everything is going well at university?"

"Fine."

"Good."

"My time is almost up."

184

"I know. It passes too quickly. At least we'll be able to catch up on everything when you come home for Christmas."

There was a pause. For a minute Wynn thought Mrs. Green had cut them off.

"Yes . . . well . . . we need to talk about that," her voice finally came back across the wires. "I may not make it home after all. Boyd has asked that I stay, and I've been thinking . . . I'd kind of like to give them Christmas this year. I mean a real one. They haven't had one, you know, since his mother died, and he can't even remember that. It's sad.

"But I have to go—we'll talk about it later. Love you, Dad. Bye."

He managed a "Love you, too," before the phone clicked, then hummed. Mutely he stood with the receiver in his hand. He wished he hadn't called. How could he tell Elizabeth that their daughter might not be coming home for Christmas either?

———

The next day the post brought a letter from Henry. As difficult as it was to wait, Elizabeth put it up on the small shelf by the radio until Wynn returned home for the noon meal. He was hardly in the door be-

185

fore she told him of it.

"What did he say? Will he be home?"

"I waited for you."

"You should have gone ahead—"

"We don't get many letters from the children. I thought we should share it."

Wynn nodded, smiled, and gave her a hug. "Should we wait until after we've eaten?" he asked, his voice teasing. But she was already on her way to get the envelope.

Elizabeth slit it open carefully and read aloud.

Dear Dad and Mom,

I've been putting off getting in touch until I had things worked out here. Regretfully I will be unable to get home for Christmas. It's too far to travel for such a short time. There are just the three of us, and Rogers needs some family time, and Laray hasn't had much experience, so I figure I'd better stay in place. I sure will miss you.

Otherwise things are going quite well here. I'm beginning to feel at home in the church. I wish it were possible for me to attend every Sunday. It's hard to get involved when one is there only now and then.

*I did start sort of a Boys' Club, though,
for eight- to twelve-year-olds. We don't do
anything too exciting. Just go on hikes and
fish a bit, etc. They seem to think it great,
though. It reminds me of your Sunday
school group, Dad. The boys want an hon-
est-to-goodness camping trip in the spring.
I promised them I'd think about it.*

*Rogers did put me in touch with a real
estate agent who finally managed to find a
little place for me. It's not much. Only a
couple of rather shabby little rooms, but it
does have a stove and I can make my own
meals. I still go down to Jessie's with the
fellows now and then, but at least my poor
stomach is getting a break.*

*I've had some more Sunday dinner in-
vitations, and believe me they are greatly
appreciated. At least most of the time. I've
been in a few houses where the woman
couldn't cook worth a nickel and a few others where the daughter was a bit too forward. But all in all I've welcomed the
change from what Jessie or I can scrape up.*

*I was wondering, Dad, if you have
been able to get any of that root for arthritis
that we talked about. Poor Mr. Martin
seems a little worse each time I see him. It's
sad because he's really not that old.*

Trust you are both keeping well. You are in my daily prayers.

With my love,
Henry

Elizabeth folded the letter slowly. She thought she had prepared herself for the possibility that Henry would not be able to make it home. But it did not seem to have lessened the keen disappointment she was feeling.

"No word about the young woman," Wynn commented.

"What young woman?" Elizabeth's attention returned to the present.

"The young widow and her son."

"I suppose there was nothing to say," said Elizabeth with a sigh. She had no idea why Wynn should mention her. What did she have to do with Henry? The long-ago accident in the North had no bearing on him now. Did it?

Suddenly she turned to her husband. "What exactly did Henry tell you about that widow?"

"Not a lot."

"Then why did you ask about her?"

"I told you at the time. Henry was

188

deeply affected by it all. It had bothered him for months. Years."

"A death such as that would."

"It wasn't only the death. It was the . . . circumstances. The young woman. The baby. It's tough to explain, Beth, but when you are the one who has to take the news, you somehow . . . share the pain. Yet you are . . . cut off. Not allowed to grieve with the family. It . . . it sort of ties you together in some unexplained way . . . yet holds you apart. It's an odd mixture of responsibility and desire to help. Finding her again—"

"He found her again?" Elizabeth interrupted. "You mean she is living in the same town as Henry?"

"Well, yes, I thought I'd told you. . . ." Wynn's voice sounded uncertain as he paused in thought. "Henry told me about it in a phone call." He paused again. "Well, anyway, it's not often that lives crisscross like that, but I get the feeling Henry still feels he owes her and the boy something. Still wants to help."

Elizabeth nodded. "It must put one in an awful position," she nodded. "I hadn't realized how personal it could become."

"Maybe it will make it easier knowing

that she has family. At least she's not all on her own."

Elizabeth agreed, but she was still troubled as she went to serve the soup. When she returned, she was feeling a little better and said, "I'll thank you, Wynn Delaney, to not forget to tell me important pieces of information about our children." He ducked in mock fright, and they both laughed.

———

The herbal medication finally arrived by a carrier who came from the North. The Indian chief to whom Wynn had appealed seemed most proud that someone of Wynn's stature and experience would ask for medicine from his tribe. He sent out a good supply. Wynn packaged it up immediately and mailed it off to Henry.

"There really aren't any directions with this," Wynn wrote, "but if I remember correctly, they made their tea with boiling water, which they drank morning and evening. They used a good-sized pinch in each cupful. Sometimes I saw them drink more than one cup at a time, but usually it was just the one. Sure hope this helps your friend. Joe Beaver Tail says it will take three full moons (and you know how long that is) before the man will know if it helps. But he's not to quit taking it then. It doesn't mean the arthritis has been cured. It just means the medicine has it under control. If he thinks it helps, they are willing to send him more. We'll pray that it helps. Love, Dad."

CHAPTER 13

A winter blizzard was sweeping across the prairies when the call came in to the RCMP office. Due to poor visibility, there had been a motor accident on one of the local roads. The caller had little further information to provide. "He just banged on my door and asked me to phone the police," she said, her voice trembling. Pencil in hand, Henry took all the information he could gather. When he hung up, he turned to his two junior officers, who had heard only his half of the conversation. "An accident. Out near the Double Bar Ranch."

"Anyone hurt?"

"The caller didn't know."

Both men were already on their feet. "That's open country. Be a miracle if we can find our way there in this storm."

"We've got to try."

All three reached for winter jackets and fur hats. Henry appreciated the fact that both his men responded immediately in spite of the risks.

"Someone needs to stay here in case we're needed," he now said. "Laray—that's been your patrol area. You come with me."

It was pitch black, and the snow was driving hard. As they left the town, they found themselves guessing as to where the road was. It was even worse when they reached open country.

"This is when I think the Force should've never given up their horses," noted Laray.

Henry had to agree. "What we really need is my dog team," he responded.

"Dog team? Yeah. What did you do with yours?"

"No one told me I'd need one here on the prairie. I left the team with the Hudson Bay trader at my last posting."

They were talking to try to cover some of the tension they felt. Someone was out there in that storm who needed their assistance. Would they make it? It was a sobering thought.

"This isn't going to work," said Laray,

staring out into the whirling whiteness. "I can't even see the trees on the side of the road."

Henry fought grimly to keep the slow-moving vehicle on the track. He felt blinded and disoriented. The swirling snow swept across the windscreen in mesmerizing fury.

"What do you remember from this road, Laray? Anything?"

"It's about eleven miles to the ranch. You need to swing off to the left about a mile and a quarter from town. There's a coulee about half a mile further. And a bridge. Wooden. Over the creek. There are some scrub willows along the road for about half a mile, then it's wide open. Wind sweeps through there like there wasn't even a cactus to slow it down."

"Any fences?"

"A few. Yeah. Lazy-Eight has some fence lines. So does that little farm that sits up against the butte. Then the Double Bar has fences around part of their property— not all of it. All together they ranch about three sections, I think. Never really figured it out."

"Any steep hills or ditches?"

"There's a couple of good dips. Straight

edge on one of them. You don't want to mess with it."

"How far?"

"It's a few miles from the farm site."

"Any buildings where we might catch a light? Windows? Anything?"

"Usually. Yeah. But I don't know in this soup. Be a miracle if anything shows up. I'll roll down the window and stick my head out. See if I can catch any glimpses of the ditch. Watch for anything that might give us a landmark."

Laray leaned out as far as he could.

The heavy swish of the wiper laboring against the snow along with the howling wind through Laray's open window limited their conversation.

"You sure we shouldn't be walking?" Laray asked after a while. "I can't see a thing out here."

"Snowshoes. Wish I had my snow-shoes."

"Snowshoes wouldn't show you the way."

Henry clamped his jaw tight and fought the car against the wind.

"Hey—slow down," called Laray. "I think this might be our corner."

Henry wondered how they could possibly go any slower.

"It is. Yeah—I see the corner post. You've got to make a turn to your left. Easy. Easy. Not quite yet. Now. Turn it easy. A little more. I think we made it."

Laray ducked back in. "That's the first hurdle," he said, sounding excited. "Now if we can just follow this road."

They crawled along, mile after mile. The storm did not slacken, and the snow on the road increased. Henry felt the car slipping sideways and fought for control. Ahead loomed the worst part of the road, and they were already fighting just to stay on it.

"Laray," Henry said. "You ever done any praying?"

"Not since I was a kid. I let my mother do the praying for me, sir."

"I think it might be wise for us both to do some now," he said, not just in idle jest.

They found themselves in the ditch. "Oh-oh. I think we've done it," called Laray. "We're awfully close to some fence posts here." He climbed out and put his shoulder to the back of the car as Henry fought to get the car back up on the road. They both breathed a sigh of relief when the wheels were able to respond.

"You see anything you recognize?" Henry asked as Laray climbed back inside.

"I hardly know what to look for. You lose all sense of distance in this white whirl," he answered, shaking the snow out of his face. "Would it be any faster if I ran along in front?"

"Appreciate your offer, but let's just hang on for as long as we can. That wind would be pretty hard to buck, and I wouldn't want to take a chance on losing sight of you."

"Don't want to drop over that edge," he warned.

"Are we getting close?"

"I've lost all track," he said, swearing softly. "Sorry, boss, about the language, but I've no idea where we are."

By some miracle the car clung to the road as they struggled onward against the storm. More than once Henry breathed an earnest prayer. They would be of no help to the accident victims if they ended up in one themselves. He was glad for a praying mother and father. And Laray had said that he let his mother do the praying. Perhaps they were surrounded by even more prayers than he knew.

Laray hoisted himself up to lean out the window again. "Whoa," he said, letting the breath out in a gasp. "We just passed over that drop-off. We missed the edge by about a foot."

Henry felt the tension in his chest. So close. Yet still going.

"We shouldn't have much further to go now. Not if it's by the Double Bar."

Through the storm a dark shape suddenly loomed before them. Henry hit the brakes and skidded sideways. He was sure they were going to hit whatever it was, but the car jerked to a stop just short of the shape that showed through the whiteness. Soon other shadows began to move around them. People running, waving arms, and all trying to talk at once.

Henry reached down to turn off the ignition. Already Laray was sprinting from the car.

Henry zeroed in on the man closest to him and called out above the howling wind, "Take us to the site. What's the situation?"

"This way," the fellow called back. "Over here."

Two trucks had collided in the storm.

One had been sent reeling into the ditch and landed on its side. The other, though upright, was the most damaged. Henry winced. Certainly there were injuries. How would they ever get them to a hospital?

"How many people?" he asked as he closely followed the man who led the way.

"Three. A couple of young cowboys from the truck in the ditch and a farmer in the other." Henry was glad no women or children were involved.

"Anyone badly hurt?"

"Could have been worse. One guy has some pretty bad head cuts. He's up walking around. Couldn't keep him down. I think the farmer has a broken leg. We laid him in the back of that truck and pulled a tarp over him. Got 'em both over there. The other fella—I don't know. He keeps saying his head hurts. That's all I can get from him. My son here and me heard this crash all the way to the barn where we were tending stock. Came on down to check it out."

"You the one who phoned for help?"

"No, I sent my boy. Over to the neighbors. We don't have a phone."

They had reached the truck where the man was lying under the tarp. Henry heard him groan before they even reached him.

Laray was already studying the one with the cuts.

Henry did a cursory examination of the leg. It was broken all right. The man would need to be moved—soon—or he'd be freezing as well. Henry turned to the farmer who'd given what help he could. "You say you live close?"

"Right over there." He pointed with his beard.

"Can we get them over to your house?"

"You're welcome to do that. The boy and I couldn't handle all three alone, and we didn't dare leave them."

"You don't happen to have a sled?"

"Kids have a small one."

"Can you send the boy for it, please?"

All the time they were talking Henry was checking the man with the head pain. He removed his gloves and let his fingers slide over the skull and neck. Dare they move him? Yet they had no choice. If left where he was, he would soon freeze to death.

He spoke to both men now. "Just hang on. We're going to get you out of here. Get you in where it's warm." He took off his heavy jacket and wrapped it around the man's upper body. The wind bit and tore at his shirt. Even heavy underwear could not hold the cold at bay.

Laray was at his elbow. "Don't think the guy's cuts are serious. Don't seem to be too deep. He's bled a lot, but head cuts always do. At least he can still walk. He should be thankful for that."

"So should we," said Henry, his voice low. "We've got to somehow get these two over to that farmhouse on a kid's sled."

They managed it. It wasn't easy, but they did it. One at a time through the storm. The boy, who turned out to be a strapping young lad whom Henry had seen in town on a few occasions, did the pulling. Henry walked beside the most seriously injured man, trying to ease the bumps and the jolts as best he could. Laray stayed with the other fellow until the sled returned. They would all be glad to get in out of the wind.

The house was small, but the woman who met them at the door quickly put everything she had at their disposal. Henry noticed that she was very relieved to have her husband and son safely back inside. From somewhere in a back room a baby cried. He heard another young voice trying to comfort the infant.

They brought every lamp in the house

to shine on the accident victims. Even so, Henry could not determine the seriousness of the head injury. He dared not give the man anything for pain. The woman worked with cold compresses on his forehead, hoping to somehow ease the throbbing.

They knew one another by name. Henry was sure that at least helped ease some of the trauma for the man. However, it also made the farm family more concerned.

"We've gotta get us over to that phone and let their folks know they're here," said the farmer.

"I'm not sure anyone should be going back out in that storm," cautioned Henry. The woman looked at her husband, eyes pleading with him to heed the warning.

"I'll ride ol' Barney. He's got a nose like a bloodhound."

"If you are intent upon going, could you call the office and let my man know we made it?" Henry requested. "And take your rifle just in case you need to signal for help." The words were more to reassure the woman than to help the farmer.

Ol' Barney must have done his job, for before they had even gotten everyone settled as comfortably as possible, the man was back.

"Got aholt of yer ma, Davey," he said. "She was mighty glad to hear you're all safe."

"Thanks," mumbled the young man with the broken leg. He was still damp with sweat in spite of his chill. Henry had needed to straighten the leg and bind it as best he could. Now the woman was busy spooning warm soup into the lanky lad.

It was the other man who most concerned Henry. He needed a doctor, but to try to get to one in the storm would be foolhardy. Henry prayed the storm would blow itself out before it was too late. He accepted a cup of the hot coffee the oldest girl was passing around to the huddled group and lowered himself to the floor, his back up against the wall. He looked across the room at Laray. The young fellow was going to make a great Mountie. He had handled himself well under pressure. Henry was proud to have him as a member of his detachment.

———

No one in the house that night got much sleep. The woman did go to bed, but Henry was sure with all the extra people and commotion in her kitchen she couldn't have rested well. She had shared some of the blankets from her bed with her unexpected guests. Even through the walls of the little farm home, the coldness of the wind could be felt.

Henry took it upon himself to keep the fires going. He hoped there was plenty of wood stacked up outside. If the storm continued much longer . . .

He must have dozed off, and he awoke with a start. He quickly rose to check on the three accident victims. The man with the cuts appeared to be sleeping without too much trouble, but the other two seemed restless.

To Henry's great relief, the sun's rays woke him the next morning. Snow still whirled about in the gusts of wind, but the storm itself had subsided. Now they had to get the injured to the hospital. It might take a long time with the roads being drifted over. They would likely have to shovel their way along. He hoped everyone would be able to stand the trip.

The farmer and his son went with them, shovels in hand, to dig out the police vehicle. With four of them, it didn't take too long to clear a path. But the motor that had sat out in the storm refused to start.

"I've got a good team and a sleigh," offered their host.

Henry nodded. It would be slow—far too slow. But at least it might get them to where they could find other help.

The man harnessed the team while Henry prepared the injured for travel. They would be taking two to the hospital. The man with the cuts insisted he would heal up on his own. Henry did not argue for long. The fellow looked much better after the blood was washed from his face.

Laray forked hay onto the sleigh to make a bed of sorts. They covered the men with borrowed blankets and spread more hay over the top. If at all possible, they hoped to keep the motionless limbs free of frostbite.

They had been on the road for less than an hour when they met a truck. Henry flagged the driver down and explained their situation. He offered to transport the men to the town hospital. The men, hay, and blankets were transferred to the truck bed. The farmer returned on home with his team, carrying words of deep gratitude to his family.

They had to shovel their way through drifts a good many times, and Henry was more than glad to see the buildings of the town appear on the horizon. It was an enormous relief to turn the injured over to the doctor's care. They had done what they could. Henry prayed silently that it might be enough.

CHAPTER 14

"I hear you're going to give us a real Christmas," Mr. Kingsley remarked as Christine laid a sheaf of papers on his desk.

She nodded, smiling.

"I can't tell you how excited Boyd is about it."

I wish my mother was, thought Christine with a little inward pang. Elizabeth had been quiet on the phone when Christine had discussed her plan. The girl knew her mother was keenly disappointed that she wouldn't be with her own family, especially when Henry wouldn't be there either. . . .

"So what do you need?" Mr. Kingsley's question intruded on her thoughts.

"I beg your pardon?"

"I assume real Christmases cost money. How much do you need?"

"Oh no," Christine hurried to explain. "It's not about money." Then she quickly realized that, yes, it was—in a way. She flushed slightly. "Well . . . you're right . . . of course. There will be some things—"

"Like?"

"Well . . . a tree. We need a tree. Our family always just trekked out and cut one. I've no idea what you do here in the city."

"Don't think the neighbor will take too kindly to us cutting down one of his," joked the big man. "What else?"

"Well . . . decorations. We always made our own, but I have seen some lovely ones in the stores."

"And. . . ?"

Christine felt her cheeks flaming. It was sounding like she really wouldn't be doing the boss and his son a favor by imposing her idea of Christmas on them.

"Look—we don't need to do this if . . ."

"No, no." With a wave of his hand he motioned her to continue. "Boyd is excited about it. He doesn't even remember a Christmas. I never bothered with one—except the gift thing. I always gave him a gift." He looked at her expectantly.

"Well, there's the meal . . . but I'll—"

"No, you won't. I happen to know what

you earn. You can't afford to go buying turkey and trimmings. Tell you what. You make out a list, and I'll take you shopping. How's that?"

Christine smiled.

"We'll get the doodads for that tree at the same time. How's Saturday afternoon?"

"Saturday is fine. Just fine."

"Good. I'll pick you up—no, you catch the streetcar. I'll meet you at the Hudson's Bay Company store. Two o'clock. Agreed?"

"Fine."

"I'll see you at two. At the west entrance."

Christine nodded.

Mr. Kingsley was more than generous. He purchased so many fancy decorations for the tree that Christine wondered if they could find one with enough branches to hold them all. All the while he kept making remarks like, "I think Boyd would like that," or "Boyd's favorite color," or "Do you think Boyd would think this pretty?" Christine got over her nervousness and threw herself into the shopping, adding garlands and wreaths to the fast-growing stack. After all, it was not for her—it was for Boyd. Mr.

Kingsley was used to spending money to keep his boy happy.

At the grocer's, Christine's list was soon completed, and more items kept appearing on the counter. "Wouldn't this taste good with turkey?" Mr. Kingsley would ask and stack something else on the pile. *We'll never get all this home on the streetcar,* Christine cautioned silently, but when it came time to settle the bill, the man simply said, "Deliver it to this address," and they left the store.

Christine debated whether to have everything done to greet Boyd when he arrived or to wait and let him get in on the fun of decorating. She decided to wait. She was sure he'd love to be involved. She carefully stacked all the bags and boxes of ornaments and longingly eyed the large tree that Mr. Kingsley had brought in. It would be hard to wait. But then—it was hard to wait for Boyd to arrive home anyway.

He arrived late Thursday night. Christine did not see him until after work on Friday. He'd slept all day, he admitted with a chuckle. He was absolutely tired out.

"When are you moving over?" he soon asked.

"Moving over? What do you mean?"

"Well—you can't do everything from here."

Christine had not even thought of changing her residence. "Oh, I'm sure I can. All I need to do is decorate and cook."

"That doesn't sound like a real Christmas," he grouched. "A cook coming in for a couple of hours."

"I'm sorry. I didn't know you'd see it that way."

He was going to sulk again.

"I thought we were going to be . . . like family."

She took his hand. "We will. I'll spend most of Christmas Day with you. I won't only be cooking."

He still didn't cheer up. Christine had learned that it was no use trying to talk him out of one of his moods. "Look," she finally said, "you likely need some more sleep. We have all Christmas vacation to catch up. And we have that tree to decorate tomorrow."

He shrugged.

"I'll see you then. It'll be fun." She stood on tiptoe and placed a kiss on his cheek.

And by the next morning, all was sunshine and warmth again. They did have fun. Boyd, going from serious and artsy to playful and ridiculous, hung decorations all over the front hall and living room. "We need more for the dining room," he exclaimed. "The store's still open. Let's run uptown and get some."

Christine laughed. "We nearly bought out the store on our first trip."

But they went for more. Christine had to admit that the house did look wonderful. Boyd had rearranged a few pieces he had hung to get a laugh and now put them in more appropriate places. Christine was pleasantly surprised to learn that he had an artistic bent. Their tree looked glorious, to Christine's thinking, because of Boyd. He tucked this in here, adjusted that ornament there, and put ribbons and streamers in all the right places.

"You're good at this," Christine complimented.

"Had you any doubt, madame?" was his response as he cocked his head to one side and swept out an arm.

———————

From his favorite chair by the crackling fire, Mr. Kingsley chuckled between sips of the hot cocoa Christine had prepared. They had spent Sunday afternoon and evening together, and she knew Boyd's father was more than pleased to have his son home.

"Oh my." Christine's smile quickly disappeared as she noticed the clock. "I have to get home. Mrs. Green will be locking the door."

The joy of the evening evaporated in an instant. She could read it in Boyd's face. Could sense it in the stirring of the big man in the chair. "This is so stupid," Boyd grumbled and threw the last bit of garland he was holding into a corner.

He turned to her, his expression stiff and cold. "You don't have to let Mrs.—Whoever run your life."

Please, thought Christine, begging him silently. *Not now. Not here in front of your father.*

She turned and went for the coat she had left in the closet off the kitchen. If he was not prepared to drive her, she'd take the streetcar. But she knew that would make her late. The streetcar, with its many stops, was much slower than Boyd's auto.

It was Mr. Kingsley who followed her out. It was Mr. Kingsley who drove her home. He made no comment about the situation, for which Christine was thankful. She was not ready either to accuse or ex-

213

cuse Boyd for his behavior.

The next morning a beautiful poinsettia was on her desk. The card read simply, *Merry Christmas. Love, Boyd.* Christine knew from experience this was his way of saying he was willing to forget all about the little incident. She guessed she was too. After all, wasn't one supposed to forgive and forget? She could not expect Boyd to be perfect.

The office stayed open until noon on the twenty-fourth. Christine's head was buzzing with things that needed to be done in preparation for Christmas Day. She hurried home, changed her office dress, and caught the streetcar to the big house. She had been busily working for almost an hour when Boyd made an appearance. "I see the cook has arrived," he said with a yawn. With his hair mussed and face unshaven, he looked as if he had just crawled out of bed.

"Do you have any juice—or anything?"

Christine nodded, wiped her hands on her apron, and found him some orange juice.

He took the glass and sat on a stool at the counter. Reaching up to run a hand through his hair, he swore under his breath. Christine realized he used such language, but rarely did he speak those kinds of words in front of her. She felt shock and deep disappointment.

He drained the juice in one long gulp. "So what's for dinner? I'm starved," he asked, wiping his mouth with the back of his hand.

"Dinner is tomorrow." Christine gave the piecrust she was working a firm thump.

"So what do we eat today?"

Christine shrugged. Then she chided herself. She was acting every bit as immature as he was. She forced a smile, willing herself to change the mood in the room. "I'm the cook for tomorrow," she said lightly. "I guess you and your father will need to figure out today. You'll manage just fine. You've had lots of practice."

He growled, "He won't even be home until who knows when. All he ever does is work."

When she didn't respond, he stood. "Well—if food's up to me, I guess I'd better go shave. Even the Greasy Spoon won't let me in looking like this."

Christine was relieved to hear a lighter note in his voice.

"By the way," he asked as he exited the room, "did the flowers arrive okay?"

"The poinsettia plant—yes. Thank you. It's beautiful."

He nodded, then was gone.

Later he returned, clean-shaven and immaculate—one would never know he could look as tousled as he had earlier, Christine noted as she lifted a golden mincemeat pie from the oven.

"Umm. You really expect that to still be here tomorrow?" His voice was teasing.

She set the pie on the cooling rack and turned to him. "It'd better be," she warned, teasing him back.

He laughed and crossed to her, removing the potholders from her fingers and lifting her hands up around his neck.

"I've been thinking. One thing we sure missed is the mistletoe." He lifted her chin and looked into her face. "But then . . ." he continued, "who needs mistletoe?" He pulled her closer and kissed her.

"What's happening tonight?" he asked against her hair.

"Go to service."

"Service?" He pushed back and looked at her. "On Christmas Eve?"

"Yes, the Christmas Eve service." She was sure she had misunderstood something. At his "What's that?" she found it hard to believe he was serious. Had he truly never been to a Christmas Eve service before? No wonder he had not been touched by the Christian faith.

She eased herself back from his arms. "It's wonderful. You'll see. It gives life—meaning—to Christmas."

He frowned.

"It starts at nine and—"

"Nine? What about Mrs. What's-her-name?"

"She gives us all a special privilege tonight."

His frown deepened. "Well, bully for her," he muttered.

She chose to ignore his last comment. "It will be a candlelight event. With lots of music. It's always beautiful."

"Like a . . . a concert?"

"More than that."

"Do they preach at you?"

She stared at him. "Preach at you? No. No, they tell the Christmas story."

"The Christmas story?"

"About Jesus' birth." Was he actually this ignorant concerning Christmas?

"Oh, that," he said with a shrug.

So he did know something about it.

He reached in his pocket and pulled out

car keys, jingling them in his hand. "Boy," he said—and Christine was not sure he was even speaking to her—"I need a new car. This old thing . . . maybe the old man . . ." He stopped and looked at her. "Whoops— maybe *my father* will spring for one. As my Christmas present. Yeah." And then he was heading toward the back door.

Just before he opened it, he turned once more. "Just to keep things straight," he said, "I haven't agreed to go to that service of yours. I didn't even know it was part of the deal."

The door banged shut, and he was gone.

As it turned out, they did go to the service. Boyd and Mr. Kingsley picked Christine up, and they drove over to the church together. As soon as she stepped inside she felt contentment wash all over her. It was so beautiful. So peaceful. So *Christmas*.

But the feeling gradually seeped away during the service. Mr. Kingsley and Boyd were both shifting uncomfortably on the wooden pew. Neither of them seemed to know the familiar carols and stood silently, shuffling their feet, while the congregation sang. When Joseph and Mary—costumed children from the Sunday school—knocked on the door of the inn, Boyd rolled his eyes in mockery. It robbed the evening of its beauty, its poignancy. Christine found herself anxious for the meeting to end.

"Well, that was nice," said Mr. Kingsley as they left the church.

"I could do with a coffee," said Boyd.

"I need to get back," Christine reminded him.

Boyd sighed in exaggerated fashion, but he made no further comment.

With Boyd's eyes on the street ahead, he said, "So, Dad—where do you want to go for coffee?"

"The Savoy Hotel," he answered without hesitation. "They always serve mincemeat pie at Christmas."

We're having mincemeat tomorrow, Christine almost said, but she bit her tongue.

"Great mincemeat," continued Mr. Kingsley.

It was snowing softly, appropriately, as Christine stepped from the car in front of the boardinghouse. "See you tomorrow," both men said. Christine concluded that their thoughts were more on the mincemeat pie than on her or the beautiful evening and Christmas celebration. She stood and watched the car spin away. The snow silently caressed her cheeks and lashes. The streetlamp's glow highlighted the drifting flakes. "Silent night, holy night," whispered Christine. But for some reason she had not yet worked through, she did not feel that it really was.

Christine was the first to trek through the newly fallen snow to the streetcar stop the next morning. She found that childishly exciting, dragging her feet so that she made swooping arcs, wishing for snowshoes so she could make more interesting patterns. She turned once and looked back, pleased with what she had just created. If she hadn't been concerned about someone possibly watching, she would have loved to make a snow angel.

The big house was silent as she let herself in at the back door. She supposed they both were still sleeping. No one in this family was inclined to bound out of bed early to discover what was under the tree.

Christine had already placed her wrapped gifts there and had noticed a few other small packages had joined hers. She didn't suppose her gifts would seem like much to a father and son who could buy anything they wanted. But she knew she had to get them something—if it was really going to be Christmas.

She moved as quietly as she could, preparing the turkey for the oven. It was much too big a bird for three people. She wondered what Mr. Kingsley would do with it after the meal was over. Well, she would not worry about that. She was sure he could find some use for the leftovers.

Even as busy as she was, she had momentary pangs of loneliness, being so alone on this most important day of the year. She carefully worked her way through her list of duties, trying to think only ahead to the enjoyment of sharing the meal together. It was almost noon before she heard anyone.

Mr. Kingsley was the first to enter the kitchen. He greeted her, sniffed appreciatively, then asked if she'd made coffee.

Christine set about putting on the pot. Mr. Kingsley pulled up a stool and talked while he waited for the coffee to boil.

"With that new snow last night, roads were a bit slick. Boyd put a dent in his front fender. But then, he says he needs a new car anyway. Thought he could go down and pick one out. For his Christmas present, you know." He laughed good-naturedly.

"He tells me he's already got a favorite. I was thinking Ford—but not my Boyd. He has an eye for the best—that boy. Well, maybe not always the best, but at least the most expensive." He laughed, then said, "Sometimes those two things don't line up right. You ever notice that?"

Christine hadn't—but she didn't shop like the Kingsleys.

Mr. Kingsley poured his own coffee. "Don't expect the boy up for a while. We didn't get to bed very early last night, and he does like his sleep. Been that way since he was a kid. Doesn't get his sleep, he gets cranky." He moved toward the door.

"Think I'll put on a fire. A bit of a chill in the air."

"Would you like something to go with your coffee?" asked Christine. "I made some muffins and there's—"

"Maybe later. I'm sorta used to getting my eyes open with coffee first."

The nine-o'clock curfew loomed when Boyd dropped Christine off at the boardinghouse. He walked her to the door, placing an arm around her shoulders and drawing her as close as he could. The parcels she held in her arms kept them a little distance apart. "Thank you for my first Christmas. First real Christmas," he said and kissed her forehead.

Christine smiled.

"The dinner was absolutely wonderful."

He kissed her again.

"And I loved the tie pin."

A third kiss. Christine began to giggle. "I hope no one's watching."

"I don't care if they are," he said, and he kissed her once more.

"Oh yes, and my father liked his tie." Playfully he leaned to kiss her again, and she pulled away, laughing.

"Thank you—again," she said seriously, "for the beautiful bracelet. I've never had anything so special."

"You deserve lots of special things—because *you're* so special."

She could not speak, nor could she reach out to him because of her parcels, so she just smiled up into his eyes—all the promises in her heart she could not say aloud.

"I must go," she whispered.

He opened the door for her, gave her a little wave, and closed the door again. She heard his whistle as he made his way to his car.

But later, as she lay curled up to marshal body warmth until her comforter took over, she felt a strange feeling of loneliness. *Why do I feel like I've missed something? Like I—didn't even* have *Christmas? We had a more beautiful tree than I've ever had in my life. I got nicer gifts. The dinner turned out well—even the mincemeat pie. So why? I even went to the Christmas Eve service. Why?*

The answer seemed to be whispered to her in the stillness of the night. *Things . . . trimmings . . . gifts—that's not what makes Christmas.*

Christine was surprised to feel tears wetting her cheeks. Somehow—in all of the flurry—she had missed the *spirit* of the wondrous event.

CHAPTER 15

Christine saw Boyd every evening that week. He usually called and set the time first, but one afternoon he arrived at the office just as she was tidying up her desk. She looked up in surprise. He gave her a big grin and pulled a long-stemmed rose from behind his back. "I'm taking the prettiest girl I know out to dinner tonight," he announced loudly enough for all those nearby to hear. Christine flushed. She was sure she was expected to join in the little game and ask who that might be, but she couldn't make herself say the words.

"And—in case you are wondering who that might be . . ." Boyd swung on his heel. "Miss Stout, are you free tonight?"

Laughter rippled through the row of

young typists, and the stiff Miss Stout glared.

"I feared not." Boyd shook his head, obviously enjoying her discomfort. "Your calendar is undoubtedly full. Well, in that case, Christine, would you honor me?"

Christine was tempted to agree with Miss Stout. The little speech had not been in good taste. But she could not say so in front of all the office staff. She merely nodded.

He ushered her out. "Where are we going?" she asked. "I'm not dressed for dinner."

"That's why I am taking you home first. You have to tell Mrs. What's-her-name, don't you, that you won't be eating at her table tonight? And I want you to put on your fanciest attire."

"I don't have any fancy attire," objected Christine.

"Then maybe we should get you some."

Christine was horrified. She was not about to let a young man buy her clothing— even if he did appear to have more money than he knew what to do with.

"You'll look just fine in something you have," he said, giving her elbow a squeeze.

"Wear that pretty blue dress. I love what it does to your eyes."

She nodded. She'd wear the blue one.

"And pin your hair up," he added, flicking one of her curls with a finger. "No—wear it down, about your face. No pins. No clips. Nothing. I love seeing it hang free like that."

She merely nodded again. He had never told her how to wear her hair before.

He took her to a new restaurant—at least new to her. It was by far the nicest place she had ever eaten. The ambiance suited Boyd's unusual mood. Grandeur. Opulence. Patrons with furs and finery. Christine sat back and sighed deeply, enjoying the luxury and the scented candlelight and soft music. But when he suggested wine to celebrate the evening, she stiffened and shook her head.

"You might discover you like it if you'd give it a try," he prompted.

She shook her head again. "I guess we'll not be finding out." She felt a bit hurt that he continued to press when she had already made her position clear on the subject.

"Do you mind if I have a glass?"

Christine did, but she shrugged her shoulders. "Suit yourself."

He ordered wine. Then he discussed the dinner with the waiter. Christine gathered that everything would be taken care of. She leaned back against the heavy plush of the secluded booth and let her eyes roam over the surroundings.

I can quite understand how folks could get to like this, she thought.

The meal was as good as it looked. Christine really did not care for the shrimp cocktail, but she did enjoy the sauce on the leg of lamb. She tried not to think about where the meat had come from. Little lambs belonged in green flower-dotted meadows, not on dinner plates.

The dessert was a fancy kind of flambé. Christine gasped as she watched the whole bowl go up in flames, thinking the server had made some dreadful mistake. Boyd laughed.

When they had finished the meal, Boyd ordered another glass of wine and moved closer to Christine. He reached out a hand and touched a tendril of her hair. "Enjoy?" he asked, leaning toward her.

She nodded, feeling rather dreamy. "And I couldn't eat another bite," she laughed. "It's been very special. Thank you.

Is this . . . is this your going-away gift to me?"

"Going away?"

"Back to college? You aren't leaving early, are you?"

He picked up her hand and placed a kiss on her palm. "No. I'm not going early. In fact, I've been thinking . . . I don't believe I'll go back at all."

Even in her languid state, Christine was shocked.

"I've had my college kick," he explained.

"What will you do?" she had to ask even as she wondered if she should.

He leaned back a bit and took a sip from his glass. When he set it down he spoke again, still toying with her hair. "Been thinking about joining Dad. He's been rather anxious for me to get involved. I've been putting him off . . . but . . . well . . . I'm beginning to change my views."

Christine smiled at him. It would be nice to have him back home . . . so close. But she wondered if she'd be able to keep her mind on her work with him in the office.

"I've been thinking about some other things too."

"Like?" she prompted when he hesitated.

"You and me. What life would be like if we were together."

Christine's breath caught in her throat. "Are you suggesting—?"

"I'm not suggesting anything, Christine. I'm asking—begging—if I have to. I really need you. I've never met anyone like you. Please. Will you marry me, Christine?"

"Are you—?"

"Serious? I've never been more serious."

"I was going to say, 'Are you sure?' "

"I'm sure. Absolutely sure."

Christine's heart was thumping. She could not believe it. Boyd Kingsley—*the* Boyd Kingsley, every girl's dream—was actually asking her to marry him.

Suddenly she looked at him from beneath her long eyelashes and whispered, "What are the magic words?"

He seemed taken aback. "I already said please. *Please*, will you marry me?"

She shook her head. "No, the *other* magic words."

He leaned forward until his lips were almost brushing her cheek. "I love you. Really. I love you." He understood.

She took a deep breath and leaned her forehead against his chin. "In that case," she said, her heart singing, "the answer is yes."

Elizabeth was glad she was able to sit down at the table when Christine's call came.

"Oh, Mother," she exclaimed when Elizabeth answered the phone, "I couldn't wait to tell you. Guess what?" she sang over the wires. "I'm engaged."

"But . . . we don't even know him," Elizabeth protested, trying to keep her dismay out of her voice.

"He's wonderful. You'll love him."

It took Elizabeth a few moments to get her breath back. In the meantime Christine hurried on over her mother's silence. "He took me to this wonderful restaurant, and we had the most magnificent meal. And my diamond! You should see it, Mother. It's huge. All the girls are envious. And he isn't going back to school. He's going to stay right here and work for his father. We'll—"

"Slow down—please. You are going much too fast for me," Elizabeth finally was able to interject.

Christine laughed, sounding giddy with excitement.

They did eventually manage to have a two-way conversation. But even so, as Elizabeth hung up the receiver she felt shaken. She could not stand around waiting for Wynn to arrive home. She grabbed her coat, pushed the waiting meal to the back of the stove, and went to meet him.

He looked surprised when he saw her coming toward him. "This is a nice treat," he said and reached out to take her hand.

Highly agitated, she poured out the entire exchange with Christine as they walked home together.

"I'm sure he's a fine young man," he said consolingly.

"We don't even know him. And she's so young. Only eighteen."

"Lots of girls are married at eighteen. Besides—they might plan on a long engagement."

"Oh . . . I certainly hope so. Well, I don't know . . ." Her uncertainty and distress about the whole situation made her chest hurt and her head ache.

"Why don't we see if they can make a trip here?" Wynn suggested, giving her hand a squeeze.

"I already tried that. Christine says they can't right now. He'll be busy learning his father's business. I asked about Easter. She said he had already made some plans."

"We'll work out something," Wynn said thoughtfully.

They were almost home when he turned to her. "What if you go visit them? You haven't been on a trip for an age."

She brightened, then sobered again. "Christine might think I'm checking on her."

"Well. . . ?" He laughed.

She gave his hand a playful tug. Then, turning serious, she said, "I don't want to alienate her."

"I don't see what could be more natural than for a mother to visit her daughter who's planning a wedding. Don't you have lots of things to discuss?"

Elizabeth nodded. It was true. Surely she would be expected to have a part in the arrangements.

"I'll call her," she said, her heart and step lighter.

———

Christine felt she was floating somewhere above solid ground. *I'm engaged. To a wonderful, handsome, most desirable young man.* They soon would be making their wedding plans. Her mother was coming to share her joy. Life could be no better.

She glowed throughout the day, and when it came time to leave the office, she ignored the chill wind and the stinging snow and walked home with warmth in her heart.

Boyd called for her. It was the first she had seen him since he had dropped her off after their engagement dinner. The first time since they were engaged.

Engaged. The word rang in Christine's ears. There was something so magical about it. So *belonging.* They were no longer just an item. They were a couple.

"One of these days," said Boyd as he ushered her down the walk toward the waiting car, "I'm going to lead you away from Old Sourpuss and not bring you back."

She was able to laugh.

"And the sooner the better," he went on. "I hate these childish curfews. You'd think you were in grade school."

He helped her into the auto and slammed her door.

"So . . . what are we doing tonight?" she asked, sliding across the seat and up next to him. He shifted gears, then reached for her hand.

"Well . . . I thought we should plan us a wedding." He grinned.

"My mother is coming," she enthused.

"I phoned her and she phoned back to say she's coming to the city. She's excited about helping me find a dress—and all that."

He said nothing, but he squeezed her hand.

"What kind of a wedding do you want? Big? Little? Private?" she asked.

"Private? Never. I want to show you off. The bigger the better. Let's make it one grand party."

"I'll want a church wedding," she commented, watching to see how he would respond.

"Have your church wedding. I've no objection. I've always pictured myself standing up there by that—what do you call that big piece of furniture in the front?—waiting for my blushing bride to come sweeping down the aisle in that long train thing. Sure—have a church wedding. Just as long as they don't preach at us or put our name on their list or something."

"What list?"

"I don't know. Heard that all churches have a list so they know who to ding for money when they need it."

She shook her head. "Who told you that? That's silly."

"Well, I don't want my name on any list."

She looked at him and frowned, wondering if he was serious. She could tell that he was.

"No list," she said quietly.

He took her to his home, and they spent the evening before the open fire discussing plans for their future together. Mr. Kingsley was conspicuously absent. The fact that she was going to be married still seemed like a dream to Christine. Time slipped away too quickly, and she scrambled up when she saw the mantel clock.

"We've got to hurry, or I'll never make it back in time," she groaned.

"This is absolutely ridiculous." He stood to his feet, grabbing a nearby cushion as he did. He flung the pillow with all his might, straight at the fire. Christine's breath caught in her throat. The flames quickly caught one corner. He turned his back on it, and Christine rushed forward. It was too late to save the pillow. She grabbed the poker and struggled instead to get the burning mass into the fireplace, where it could cause no harm to anything else. Acrid smoke began to fill the room.

By the time she turned back, he had

snatched his coat from the hall closet and was stomping from the room. Christine took one more look at the fire to assure herself it was safe to leave, then followed him.

"That was dangerous," she said after they had ridden for many minutes in a silent car.

"This is ridiculous." His face was still contorted with anger. He made no excuse for his behavior. "How are we ever to plan a wedding when you have to be back to your room at such a ridiculous hour? The day is just getting started. Even Cinderella was given until midnight."

"Cinderella was a fairy tale," Christine reminded him.

"Well—this is no fairy tale, I grant you that. Though we do have us a wicked witch."

"Are you referring to Mrs. Green—or me?" asked Christine, turning toward him.

He pulled the car over to the curb and reached for her. "Hey," he said, reaching both hands to her hair. His anger had dissolved as quickly as it had begun.

His fingers loosened the pins, letting it spill about her shoulders. "You're no witch. You know how I feel about you. It gets harder and harder to let you go. Don't you

237

know that?" He pulled her toward him, one hand on each side of her head and kissed the tip of her nose. "I hate it when your Mrs. Green takes you away from me."

His words—his manner—were so tender, so sweet, that they tore at Christine's heart.

"I really do need to go," she whispered. "It won't be long until we . . . we won't need to be apart. Not ever."

She reached for the handle of the door, but he stopped her.

"Not yet. I can't let you go yet."

"But she will lock the—"

Her words were hushed by his kiss.

At last she pulled away, and he reluctantly let her go. Silently he walked her to the door. But she knew even before she tried the knob. She was too late. It was locked.

Without a word he turned her around and headed her back toward the car. "Good thing we've got all those extra bedrooms," he said, sounding neither surprised nor repentant. Had he delayed her on purpose? But she put the thought from her mind.

CHAPTER 16

Christine had never felt as embarrassed, as humiliated, as she did the next morning when she returned to the boardinghouse to dress for another day of work.

She knew many eyes followed her as she passed the dining area where her fellow boarders were having their breakfast. She tried to ignore them, but her cheeks flamed in spite of her effort to appear composed.

Back in the privacy of her own room, she changed her dress quickly. Mr. Kingsley, who always arrived at the office long before anyone else, was waiting in the car outside, reading the morning paper and drinking a cup of coffee he had picked up at a corner shop. Boyd, Christine assumed, was still sleeping.

Christine didn't feel prepared to face a

new day. Boyd had insisted on talking late into the evening. Christine had not entered the unfamiliar bedroom until some time after midnight. She had felt jumpy and confused—and a bit annoyed. She could not close the door on the impression that Boyd had deliberately held her back so this would happen.

She of course had not had a nightgown or toothbrush. Not even a brush for her hair. She felt so . . . so stranded, so coerced into something not of her choice. So manipulated into difficult circumstances. And he had expected her to be sweet, compliant, eager to discuss wedding plans. The rest of the evening had been very difficult.

Now he was sleeping in while she scrambled to get herself in some kind of order for a day at the typewriter. And she'd had no breakfast. Not even a cup of coffee as her boss now enjoyed. Her stomach grumbled as she pictured those around the table, eating heartily of Mrs. Green's morning porridge and toast with marmalade.

She would never be late again, she determined. Never.

Her hair did not go right, and after struggling with it she gave up and tied it back with a ribbon.

She had just stepped through her door and pulled it firmly shut behind her when she found herself face-to-face with Mrs. Green.

"Miss Delaney."

Christine nodded.

The elderly woman looked more sad than stern. "I have reason to think you didn't use your room last night."

Christine flushed but nodded.

"I . . . I was . . . detained," she stammered. "By the time I . . . the door was already locked. I . . . I stayed at a friend's house. They have extra—"

"Your father entrusted you into my care."

Christine nodded. "It won't happen again. I'm very sorry."

Mrs. Green's face had not relaxed. Somehow she looked older—drawn.

"I hope not. For if it does, I will be forced to ask you to find accommodation elsewhere, and I will notify your father accordingly. I will not take responsibility for that which I cannot control."

"I understand," said Christine in little more than a whisper. "I'm sorry to have troubled you." She felt sick inside.

The woman turned and headed back toward the kitchen, and Christine, with flushed cheeks but determined steps, made her way back past the dining room. Christine did not so much as glance in their direction or give the group her usual good-morning greeting.

Mr. Kingsley had finished his paper and his coffee and sat drumming his fingers on the steering wheel. Christine slipped in beside him. "I'm sorry," she mumbled another apology, wrapping her unbuttoned coat more closely about her body.

Mr. Kingsley did not speak for a moment. When he did, his meaning was totally obscure to Christine. "In the future I think we'll need to make some other arrangements," he said. "No need for you to be going into the office at this time of the day." He put the car in motion.

Christine had no idea what the man was referring to. "I'll just take the streetcar—as I always have," she replied.

"That won't work. You'd have to leave even earlier than this to get to work on time. Requires about three transfers. You'd see the entire city before you got to the office."

She still was not following him. "I don't do a transfer at all," she explained. "It goes straight along the street from the boardinghouse to the office. That was one reason my father chose—"

"I'm talking about *now*," he said, looking across at her. "Not what was—but how it'll be with you at our house."

Christine blinked. He assumed she had finally accepted his offer—was planning to stay from now on. Quickly she corrected his impression. "Oh—I haven't moved in. I was just too late for the door last night. But I've no intention—"

He looked surprised. "Boyd said—"

"No," said Christine insistently, shaking her head. "Boyd must have misunderstood."

"He plans to go over after work today to gather all your things. He asked me if you could get off work early so you could pack up."

"We never even discussed it," said Christine, and suddenly she felt hurt and angry. Why would Boyd make such plans knowing how she felt?

"He plans to phone that—whatever her name is—your landlady today to tell her—"

"He can't," cut in Christine, feeling sudden panic.

Mr. Kingsley was scratching his head under the brim of his hat, making it wriggle in a cartoonish fashion. Christine wished he would put both hands back on the wheel. The slippery streets made her nervous.

"I just spoke with Mrs. Green," she told him firmly. "I have no intention of moving out."

He turned his head again and looked at her, making her more nervous. "Well—I've no idea how things got so balled up. Seems to me it would make a good deal more sense to do it Boyd's way. You'll be married in a few months. What difference—?"

"There's lots of difference," Christine argued, her cheeks feeling hot with frustration and anger. "We aren't married *now*. My folks would be very disappointed if I left the place my father had found for me."

"Seems a little old-fashioned."

"Perhaps proper conduct always is," Christine dared to say.

They pulled into the parking lot, and Christine was glad the ride was over. Now she had to get in touch with Mrs. Green before Boyd did. She could have called Boyd before he made the call, but he was not up. Mr. Kingsley had joked about how soundly the boy slept. He would never hear the phone. But when he did get up, whatever time of the day that might be, he likely would be going through with his plan.

With shaking hand Christine rang the operator and gave her the number. Mrs. Green was soon on the other end of the line.

"This is Christine Delaney. I . . . I understand . . ." How in the world could she phrase this? It sounded ugly even to her own ears. "There's been a . . . a misunderstanding. My . . . my fiancé is . . . is thinking that I . . . that I am planning to leave your boardinghouse to live elsewhere. I've no intention of moving. None whatever. So if he should call, would you please just tell him that I will speak to him about the matter?"

Christine found it hard to settle down to her work. Her whirling thoughts on top of an empty stomach made it difficult to concentrate. Miss Stout was the first to push open the heavy door, and she looked surprised to see Christine already at her desk.

Christine had finished all her work the day before, and as no one was in to assign her new tasks—except for Mr. Kingsley, who had not called for her nor appeared at his door since it had shut behind him—she had nothing in particular with which to busy herself. She simply shuffled papers, pretending to read.

Now she greeted Miss Stout with a forced smile.

Mr. Peterson, next to arrive, came in, stamped his feet loudly, shook the snow from his hat onto the carpet—bringing a frown from Miss Stout—and announced in his raspy voice, "Snowing again."

The next two men came in together, already in deep conversation about a business account, and did not even bother to give Miss Stout a nod of acknowledgment. Her lips pursed as she looked at their retreating backs.

Christine eventually felt herself relax. Soon they could get on with their day. The other office girls would be arriving, the rhythm of their keyboards filling the uncomfortable silence of the room. Things would feel so much better when they all fell back into the usual routine.

Boyd was waiting for her when she left the office. He did not look to be in good humor, and Christine felt her stomach tighten.

He said nothing, just opened the door on the passenger side, then with a stoneface climbed in and started the engine.

They had driven for several blocks in total silence when Christine said, "We need to talk."

He did not look at her but answered stiffly with, "You're right. We need to talk."

He was not heading to her boarding-house. Nor was he taking the street that led to his home. Christine had no idea where he was going. She was hesitant to ask.

He pulled into an empty area on the brow of a hill overlooking the river and switched off the engine.

"Now," he said, straightening up, "care to tell me why you chose to make me look stupid?"

Christine's mind scrambled to try to sort out his meaning.

"I don't understand—"

"No, I don't think you do." He sounded so angry. She did not know what she had done.

"I called up to make the arrangements— just to save you the fuss—and got told in no uncertain terms that I didn't know what I was talking about. That you weren't plan-ning to move out. Do you have any idea how stupid that made me feel?"

Christine shook her head, "I didn't mean—"

"You didn't *mean?* Surely you can see how it would look. We're to be married, and you make me look like—" He said words Christine had never heard from him before. Her cheeks burned with shame—for both of them.

"I'm sorry—"

"You're *sorry?* Sorry doesn't cut it. I don't like looking stupid. Not even to that old hag."

Christine's head came up. "She's not an old hag," she declared, fire in her voice. "And she is right. I am not planning to move out. Not until I am married. It would not *look* right. It would not *be* right. My—"

Christine felt a sharp blow sting her cheek. He had struck her.

One hand went up to cover the shame and humiliation. In spite of her resolve, tears spilled out and her lips trembled.

"Now look what you've gone and made me do," he accused, but his voice had softened. He reached over to pull her into his arms. "Let's not fight," he whispered. "We can straighten this all out." He was kissing her forehead. Christine felt her body tense, stiffen in resistance. How could he strike her one minute and kiss her the next?

He seemed to be aware of her reluctance. "I'll take you home. We'll talk about this later."

He did take her home. Soon after, a large bouquet of winter blossoms was delivered along with a card that read simply, *I love you. Boyd.* Christine shook her head in confusion. Frustration.

She sat on her bed and stared at the bouquet on her dresser. An engagement was a tense time. She simply must forgive him. It would be different once they were married. She'd just need to be careful not to push him, not to make things awkward for him.

———

Elizabeth arrived when winter still clutched the town with icy fingers. Christine shivered on the train platform, thankful it was not windy.

She had not realized how wonderful it would be to see her mother. How much she had missed her. They clung together, mingling tears and exchanging little words of mother-daughter love.

"I told Boyd not to come over tonight," Christine laughed and wiped her eyes. "I want this time just for us. He's going to take us to dinner tomorrow."

Elizabeth sounded pleased with the arrangement. "I want to spend the entire evening catching up on everything that's happened over the past months," she said.

They took a cab to the boardinghouse and settled in to talk. Christine could hardly get the words out about her Boyd quickly enough, displaying the diamond ring and gifts he had given. She so much wanted her mother to approve of him and love him too.

"You'll meet him tomorrow. I can hardly wait," Christine concluded, hugging her mother again.

They talked until late into the night. After Christine had finally exhausted all the wonders of her betrothed, the conversation turned to Wynn and Henry and even Teeko.

"I still miss the North," Christine sighed. "But I like it here too," she quickly added.

———

Boyd picked them up sharply at six the next evening and took them to the nicest restaurant in town. He was a model suitor, attending to each need and desire of both ladies. Christine was proud of him. She could tell her mother was impressed.

The next night the three went out again.

Then Boyd drove them to his home so Elizabeth could meet his father. Mr. Kingsley was more than polite. He was charming. Christine had never seen him so well-groomed, attentive, and courteous.

"It's a shame you ladies have to stay at the boardinghouse with all these rooms going to waste. Certainly you both would be welcome to stay here while you are in town, Mrs. Delaney. I'm sure with our chaperoning there would be no raised eyebrows."

No, Mom, Christine cried inwardly, *don't agree to this. I'd never escape again.*

"Perhaps not," Elizabeth said graciously. "And I do thank you for your kindness, but we are rather enjoying the opportunity to share a room and woman-talk until the wee hours." Elizabeth laughed softly. Much to Christine's relief, Mr. Kingsley dropped the matter.

Saturday evening they all went out for dinner together. Mr. Kingsley was full of questions about the North and Wynn's work with the RCMP. "Fascinating! Most fascinating. You must have many stories to tell, Mrs. Delaney."

When Boyd walked them to the door of the boardinghouse, he took Christine's hand. "What time would you like to be picked up in the morning?" he asked.

"In the morning?" She tried to remember what had been said about plans for the next day.

"For the church sermon."

"Oh—the church service." Even as Christine thrilled at his words, she hoped her mother had not caught the slight misstatement.

"Ten-thirty," she said, trying to keep her voice sounding natural. "I think that will give us plenty of time."

"Fine." He smiled and bent to kiss her cheek. Christine flushed at this first time he had kissed her in front of her mother.

"Thank you once again for a very pleasant evening," Elizabeth said, extending her hand to the young man.

"My pleasure," he replied, touching the brim of his hat.

Christine felt the entire week went well—and very quickly. Mr. Kingsley even gave Christine a few days off so they might shop together. In vain they searched the stores for the perfect wedding dress. At last they settled on material and a pattern. Elizabeth would sew the gown. Her deep pleasure was evident as she looked forward to fashioning the garment that her daughter would wear on the most exciting day of her life.

Again Boyd drove them to church and even managed not to squirm much through the service. At one point, Christine cast a glance his way and found he was actually listening to what the minister was saying. She smiled to herself. God was answering her prayers. Boyd was changing. Her heart swelled with happiness. She was so blessed.

———

Elizabeth left the next morning. With tears and promises, they bid each other good-bye. It would not be long until they saw one another again. Boyd was pressing for a June wedding, and the months would go by very quickly. Henry had already scheduled the time off so he could stand up for his little sister. Christine had chosen one of the young women from the church to be her attendant. Boyd was not happy with such a small wedding party, so he had asked that his friends be included. Christine had agreed, with a bit of reservation. She had heard little of his friends over the past months. She had secretly hoped Boyd was not seeing as much of them as he once did. But he did drop little comments now and then about what one or another of them was doing or had said. Christine knew he was still in touch.

I suppose it is only right that they be included. It's his wedding too, she reasoned.

The next Sunday she dressed for church and took a seat in the hallway. She did not want to keep Boyd waiting. But the clock ticked on and on, and he did not come. At length she gave up and took the streetcar. She was quite late, which bothered her. As she neared the large oak doors, she knew she could not go in without drawing undue attention. She turned and walked to the trolley stop to catch the next streetcar back home. It was going to seem like a long Sunday without the comfort of the worship, without the pleasure of meeting her church friends. It seemed that Boyd's interest in spiritual things had already waned.

Elizabeth carried home a good report. She and Wynn spent the evening in front of a crackling fire as she shared all of her adventures in the city.

"Our daughter sounds happy," said Wynn.

"She appears to be."

Teeko stirred at Wynn's feet, yawned, and lay back down.

"Boyd certainly sounds like a fine young man."

"He was most polite and thoughtful."

"The father seems to think well of Christine."

"He rather dotes on her."

A log snapped, sending sparklers dancing upward.

"So why do I still see that doubt in your eyes?" he asked frankly, reaching out for her hand.

She clung to his offered support and took a minute to answer. "I don't know. I just . . . feel that . . . things might not be what they seemed. There was just some . . . underlying current that . . . I pray I'm wrong. But I feel more . . . more uneasy now than I did before I went."

Their prayers together that night for their Christine were even more fervent than usual.

CHAPTER 17

"Oh boy," Henry said, reading the latest dispatch as he stood in the office doorway.

"What's up?" Rogers did not lift his head from the report he was completing.

"We're going to have us a visitor."

Rogers did look up then. "Good—or bad?"

"About as bad as you can get. Short of murder. Just completed a term in prison. Was released day before yesterday. Now he's out, and they think he's on his way back here."

"You say 'back.' Is he from here?"

Henry sat down heavily and continued reading. "Has a shack along the creek someplace. This is already his third trip up with free room and board."

"Why do they let a guy like that out?"

Rogers was on his feet now, moving toward Henry's chair. He leaned on the desk and looked over Henry's shoulder. "Look at him. Look at that face. He even looks evil." Rogers picked up the paper and peered at the mug shot.

"So that's what we need to look out for?" Rogers said as he put the sheet back on the desk.

"Might be some changes. Beard—no beard. Different haircut. Those kinds of things. Even a dye job. There are lots of ways to change one's looks. But study the eyes. Can't change his eyes. Look at him. He looks—"

"Sinister," Rogers filled in.

They both studied the picture.

"Look here," said Henry. "He's got a scar along his jawline. He could almost hide that under a beard. But it would likely still show a bit—right up here."

"A scar. Left side. Yeah—he can't very well hide that."

The two perused the picture as though to memorize every line, every detail. Someone's life might depend upon it.

Henry shook his head and eased back in his chair, running a finger over his mustache.

"Man—I hate this," exclaimed Rogers, straightening. "I thought this was a nice safe little town for my wife and kids."

"I'm afraid it might not be safe for anyone with him around—especially women who might be on their own." Henry's thoughts immediately jumped to Sam. How would they manage to protect her?

"Maybe he won't show."

"I hope and pray he won't. We don't have enough men to carry on with our regular duties plus keep a twenty-four-hour vigil on a guy like that."

Rogers walked back to his desk, rubbing a hand vigorously over his head. "It would sure help if we could put folks on the alert."

"You know we can't."

"Yeah, I know. But it seems stupid to me. Here's a dangerous guy on the loose, and we have to cover for him."

"We won't cover for him. If he does show up, we're going to watch him like a hawk. He steps out of line—anything, anything at all—we nail him."

"He's likely got plenty of crime savvy. He'll take some watching."

"Then he's met his match."

But for all his assurances to Rogers, Henry felt restless. Uncertain. How could the three of them keep an eye out on the whole town and the surrounding area? It wasn't possible. He needed more detailed information on the guy. What were they up against?

His call to headquarters did not give him much additional background. Only caused him further concern. On previous occasions this man had gone after women he knew to be alone. Evening hours—between nine and midnight—seemed his preference. That was all they had to go on.

Henry could not settle back to work. He finally gave up and reached for his Stetson. "Keep an eye on things," he said to Rogers. "I'll be back shortly."

He walked slowly to Sam's, trying to get his foolish heart to stop hammering. If only there was some way—some legal way—to let her know about this possible threat to her safety.

He wasn't sure if another haircut would be questioned. It hadn't been that long since he'd had one. Could he cite warmer weather? No, his hair was never long enough to cause him any concern with heat.

Well—maybe he would think of something. Anything. Just to get a chance to talk with her. See if there was some way to alert her and make sure she remained secure.

He stepped up to the door just as it opened. Some other customer was just leaving. Henry stepped aside and nodded a greeting. The man was just putting on his hat—a beat-up, wide-brimmed black Stetson. He returned Henry's nod. Henry noted intense dark eyes just before the hat hid them from view. Immediately Henry looked at the man's cheek covered with a light growth of dark beard. There, just below the sideburn, was the ragged tail of a scar.

Henry felt as if he'd been kicked in the stomach. Their worst fear had just been realized. And the felon had already been in to pay a visit to Sam.

Henry dropped the haircut idea, turned, and headed back to the office.

———

Henry supposed that none of them were getting much sleep. The police cars were kept on the move, especially in the evening hours. Up and down streets they cruised, back and forth, over and over, watching for shadows, jumping at newspapers flying in the wind or a cat tipping over a trashcan. And not a soul in town knew of their churning stomachs, the intense fear, the wearing down of stamina.

Twice they saw the man on the streets. Twice they followed him when he left, making sure he was heading back to his place in the hills.

He drove an old beat-up, once-blue pickup, with a license plate hanging haphazardly from baling wire. A mangy dog always rode in the front seat beside him and growled deeply when anyone came anywhere near the vehicle.

"You think I could provoke that dog into an attack?" Laray wondered.

"Don't try anything that might get you hurt," warned Henry. Truth was, he had thought of it himself. "He wouldn't have to do anything more than have the dog destroyed. That wouldn't solve our problem."

The next time the convict was in town, Laray entered the office out of breath. "I just saw that there fella jaywalking. Want me to bring him in?"

Henry shook his head. Everyone in town jaywalked at one time or another. "No—they'd never hold him on that. He might have to pay a twenty-dollar fine. That's all. Just keep an eye on him. He'll trip up one of these days."

Henry wanted to believe his own words, but he was getting more and more nervous about it.

It didn't help Henry any when the next time he went for his regular haircut, he again met the fellow just coming out. This time he was grinning, and he tipped his hat to Henry.

There was little sleep after that. The three patrolled with a passion, paying particular attention to any house where they knew a woman lived alone. Jessie was offered rides home in a police cruiser if she had to close shop very late.

The officers forgot about the roster, putting in as many hours as they could manage and still function. Henry worried about Rogers's family. Those little girls must have wondered why their daddy had to be gone so much. Possibly the officer had confided in his wife. Henry thought he would have been tempted to give some kind of warning if he had a wife and baby girls at home.

Henry decided the squad car was a bit too obvious and took to walking the streets. He didn't want the whole town speculating about why they were out prowling around the neighborhood.

His circuit took him past Sam's bungalow several times a night. Always he stood on the other side of the street, hidden by a growth of caraganas, and watched and waited. His eyes looked for movement, shadows, anything that didn't belong to the night.

I'm getting downright jumpy, he accused as a night bird's call startled him.

He was about to move on when he thought he saw movement at the screen door. His stomach did some kind of a nasty flip. His heart pounding wildly, he made his way across the street and silently onto the porch. The screen door was gently rocking back and forth in the light breeze. Henry reached for the wooden door's brass knob, praying it would resist his hand. It didn't. With a soft squeak that sickened him, it turned and opened.

The house was dark and silent. But he had to know. Had to. Should he call? Should he turn on a light? No, if there was indeed an intruder in the house, he did not want to spook him. But what if the fellow already had been there and left? That thought drove Henry onward. He stumbled over some piece of furniture, chiding himself for the scraping noise it created. One

hand outstretched, he groped his way forward. He had no idea what rooms were
where.

He was about to enter another door
when he saw a movement to his left. He
stopped absolutely still, readying himself to
spring forward. A curtain shivered in the
breeze at the window, letting in a splash of
light from the streetlamp in front of the
house. Sam stood there, arm upraised, prepared to do battle with the intruder. Before
he could say a word, she flung whatever it
was she had in her hand with all her might.
He had just enough forewarning to lift his
other arm, diverting the blow from the piece
of firewood that came hurtling at him. The
end of the stick grazed his cheek. He could
feel the sting of it even as he called out, "It's
me. Delaney."

He heard her intake of breath. In the
next instant the room was flooded with
light. She stood there, breathing heavily
from fright and exertion. Her face was as
pale as her worn robe, framed by hair hanging down around her shoulders.

"What in the world do you think you're
doing?" she demanded.

"Your . . . your door was open," he said

lamely, dabbing at his cheek with his handkerchief.

"Open? It was closed when I went to bed."

"It . . . well, the screen door was swinging in the wind."

"It often swings in the wind."

She wasn't making this easy.

"When I checked it, I found the inner door wasn't locked."

"Most folks in this town don't worry about locked doors."

"Well, they should," he said firmly. "From now on I want that door locked every night."

"You have so much time on your hands you're policing doors now?" she asked, her sarcasm plain.

He moved toward the door. "Please, please," he said. "I'm asking you to do this for reasons I'm not at liberty to divulge."

She backed up a step and swallowed hard, her expression changing. "You frightened me half to death," she said, pulling her robe more tightly around her slender frame.

"I'm sorry. I didn't mean to. Sorry."

"I'm a little on edge," she admitted. "There's this guy who's been coming in for cuts lately." She shook her head. "Well, anyway—" She broke off and moved toward the kitchen. "Come in here," she said, "so we don't waken Danny. You'd better let me check your cheek."

"It's fine. Fine. A little scrape, that's all. Just—please—lock your door when I leave."

"Okay. I'll lock it."

As soon as he was back on the sidewalk he finished dabbing at the injury. It was already swelling slightly. His arm had taken quite a whack too. He shook his head; then a smile pulled at the corners of his mouth. The little lady packed a mighty wallop.

———————

"What happened to you?"

Henry had known he would be questioned. He didn't know how to be evasive, and he wasn't about to lie. "A chunk of firewood. Mistaken identity," he answered without looking up.

"So who . . . mistook you?" Laray set down his coffee cup and surveyed the bruise.

Henry kept his eyes on the map he was studying. "Well . . . Sam, actually."

He was still debating proper police protocol. Was he going to file a report on this?

"Sam? *Him* Sam or *her* Sam?"

"Her Sam."

He thought he heard a snicker, but he didn't look up to check. He figured he might as well blurt it all out since it looked like he'd be questioned to death.

"I was patrolling the street—by her house—when I saw the screen door was open. I checked. Found her other door wasn't locked. I went in to see if everything was okay and—"

"You went in?"

It sounded pretty stupid. Henry hurried on. "She thought it was an intruder—"

"Which it was," Rogers dared to say with a smirk.

"So she hit you with a chunk of firewood?" Laray sounded incredulous.

"Not hit . . . exactly. She threw it."

Now he knew they were both laughing. He did not look their way. Just went on staring at the map he wasn't seeing.

"So . . ." said Laray after a few moments of weighty silence. "You gonna arrest her for assaulting a police officer?"

"Don't be—" Henry grabbed for his Stetson and left the office amid loud guffaws. He knew it would be some time before the boys were willing to let him forget the whole incident.

They finally got a break. Laray, tailing the ex-con on another of his visits to town, caught him red-handed shoplifting a pack of cigarettes. It wasn't much—petty theft. But it might be enough to gain them a bit of time. At least a few nights of sleep. They hoped the judge, whoever it was, would be able to do a bit of reading between the lines. Find a reason to give the guy the maximum sentence the offense allowed. They all breathed a bit easier as they loaded him, handcuffed, into the back of the cruiser and gave him an escorted ride to jail.

CHAPTER 18

With spring came clamoring from the church boys to make plans for the camping trip. Henry thought it was still too early. Pockets of snow remained in sheltered places, muddy tracks in place of dry road-beds. Nights held a chill that could make one shiver, even under blankets warmed by a campfire. But the boys continued to coax and harass their parents, the pastor, and their club leader, Henry.

"Maybe Easter weekend," Henry conceded. "If we don't get another storm between now and then."

As far as the boys were concerned, this was a promise. They began to plan with renewed vigor. Henry soon had thirteen boys ready to pack up knapsacks and head for the hills.

Henry had just emerged from the morning service when he felt a tug on his coattail. He turned to find Danny, face flushed with eagerness, looking up at him.

"Can I go too? Please?"

With all his heart Henry wished to say yes. But he knew it was not his decision. "Well, now," he said, looking around for Danny's mother. "I'm afraid I can't decide that, Danny. Your mother will need to give you permission."

"Would you ask her? Please. I asked her and she said I was too little."

Henry did not know how to answer the young boy.

"Please," the child begged further. "Papa Sam thinks I'm big enough."

"Maybe Papa Sam should talk with your mother."

"She needs to know from you," he said with a child's intuitive perception. "What you will do on the camping trip. What we need to take along. All that stuff."

Henry nodded, wondering just what he was getting himself into. "I'll give it a try," he said and ruffled the boy's hair. He noticed again how like his mother's it was in color.

"Thanks." Danny looked confident and excited.

Henry squatted down on Danny's level and looked him in the eye. "Remember, Danny, I said I'd *try*. Your mother could have some very good reasons for saying no—"

But Danny was already scampering away with a great deal of hope on his face.

Henry stood to his feet, his mind grappling with the challenge facing him. He had no idea how to approach her. She had obviously avoided him since the incident with the firewood. In fact, other than a curt nod on Sunday mornings, they had not exchanged a greeting. Already he had stretched the days between haircuts longer than he should have. He reached up to feel the nape of his neck before placing his hat on his head. He would not be able to put off the cut much longer.

But even as he walked down the steps to the sidewalk, nodding at the two Miss Walkers as he did so, he knew it would not be wise to try to discuss the matter with her when in the barber chair. There were usually others who came in for their turn, and there was no need for the town to be in on the conversation.

He thought about dropping by her parents' home and requesting their intervention on Danny's behalf. Surely they could be more persuasive than he would be—and likely more successful.

He discarded that idea as well. He had assured the child that he would do it, and Danny was depending on him.

He rang her phone as soon as he reached home from church. "Sorry to bother you on a Sunday, but there's a little matter I would like to discuss. Would it be possible to meet for a few minutes?"

There was a pause, then, "Not more intruders—I hope. I *am* locking my door."

He couldn't tell from her voice how she meant the comment. "Good," he decided was a safe response. "That's not what I wish to discuss, however."

He could hear a sigh over the line.

"All right. When?" she agreed.

"That's up to you. For my part—the sooner the better."

"Okay," she said. "This afternoon?"

"That would be fine. What time?"

"About four?"

"Four? Sure. That's great."

He was about to hang up when he thought of something else. "Look," he said, "could we have this discussion without Danny present?"

"Well . . . why?" She seemed to struggle for comprehension.

"I . . . I really can't say now. It's just . . . I think we'll be a little freer to talk—openly—if he isn't around."

Her silence probably indicated she didn't like the idea.

"I thought maybe he could spend a little time with your folks," he hurried on.

She finally said, "All right."

"I'll come by at four. We can go—"

"No. No, that won't be necessary. We can say anything that needs to be discussed on my front porch."

"Very well."

He couldn't help being disappointed. He had fleeting mental pictures of a drive in the country. Maybe a stop for a cup of coffee. The leaves were starting to uncurl fingers of green; the grasses were peeking up from the winter's brown. Meadowlarks were calling from grayed fence posts. He thought this could be a chance. . . .

Well, anyway, he knew better than to argue. "See you at four, then."

The click as she hung up the receiver resounded in his ear with symbolic finality.

This is not going to work, thought Henry, rubbing a hand through his hair. *Poor little kid. She won't even let him be a boy. . . .*

But he knew he was disappointed for more reasons than for Danny. She had delivered another clear signal. She wanted nothing to do with him. For a moment he wished he had never been transferred to this detachment, had never seen her again. But he immediately knew that was a lie. The relief to know she was getting along all right was worth every minute of her resolute distance from any offer of friendship.

He decided not to cook his own meal after all and grabbed his hat again. Jessie's Sunday grub might burn all the way down, but a little company would sure beat time spent agonizing over the situation.

Time dragged until four o'clock. Twice he started toward his door, then made himself sit down again. He did not want to be early. She would view any sign of eagerness with suspicion.

Promptly at four he arrived and rapped. She answered immediately. He wondered if she had been waiting for the knock, then quickly chided, *Of course she's waiting.* She had probably been uncomfortable all afternoon, knowing it was coming.

Danny was nowhere in sight.

She nodded her head toward a willow-branch set of chairs on the porch. He removed his hat and took one. It creaked slightly when he lowered himself into it. "Nice chair," he commented, running his hand over the worn-smooth surface of the arm.

She took the other chair, pulling a light wrap around her.

"Seems like spring is really here to stay," he observed. "Saw my first bluebird the other day. You might fool robins occasionally, but you rarely fool bluebirds."

She said nothing.

"Creek's acting up a little bit," he tried again. "We're going to have to watch it from now on. The mountain thawing could swell the stream."

She stirred. "Look—I know you didn't come here to talk about chairs or spring."

He sat up straighter, making the willow complain again. "No. No," he said, reaching up self-consciously to rub his mustache.

"So what did you come here to talk about?"

"Danny," he said abruptly.

She straightened visibly. "Is . . . is he in

trouble?" Her voice seemed to catch in her throat.

"Danny? Oh no. What trouble could he possibly be in?"

"I've no idea, but . . ."

Henry heard the worry of a mother in her tone and felt sorry he had given her any cause for concern. "Danny's a great kid," he said with feeling. "You don't need to worry about him."

"Then why—"

"He asked me to."

That seemed to slow her down—and bring a frown to her smooth forehead.

He knew he had to state his case quickly. Get it all out where she could mull it over and hopefully understand how important this was to her small son.

"He heard about the camping trip," he said quickly. "Everyone's heard." He managed to smile. "Those boys talk of nothing else."

"And—?"

"He wants to go."

He heard her intake of breath and knew she was going to say no without even thinking about it. He stopped her with a raised hand. "Before you say anything, please let me tell you about it. There are a dozen boys

276

or more and two dads. We'll be gone only one night. They'll fish a little, sleep out under the stars, eat campfire food, and think they've been on a real adventure."

"He's too young," she said immediately.

"Taylor is bringing his boy. He's the same age as Danny."

"Taylor can do what he wants."

"But Danny and Ralph play together—"

"That doesn't mean they have to camp together."

He rubbed a hand over his chin. He knew he was getting nowhere.

"Danny might be young. But he'll be well supervised. I'll take responsibility myself." Even as he spoke the words he knew his explanation would not be good enough.

"You'll be busy with a dozen boys."

"That doesn't mean I can't keep particular watch on Danny."

"Look," she said, her voice cold. Strained. "Ralph Taylor will have his father. It'd be different if—"

"I'd look after Danny the same way."

"No—no, you wouldn't. You're not his father. You can't possibly act that way. Don't you understand what a father is?"

He stood. He had lost. The poor little guy.

"Yes," he said, reaching for his Stetson. "I think I do. I was raised in a big gaggle of tough siblings. I was the youngest—and the lowest in the pecking order. My father—for that's what I was told he was—thought far more of the bottle than of his brood. I was frightened of him. All I knew was to stay as far out of his reach as I could. Especially when he'd been on a bender. Then one day I met this man. He took me camping. He taught me about life—and love. He fought with every means at his disposal until I finally shared not just his home but his name. That was what I wanted. What I needed. Acceptance. Love. The right to grow up to be a man, with a role model to show me how. Now, ma'am, I ask you. Who is my father?"

He did not wait for her answer. He dipped his head in her direction as he replaced the hat and walked down the wooden steps without looking back.

The camping trip was a huge success in everyone's eyes but Henry's. Ever, in the back of his mind, were the sad eyes of the little boy when he had reported that the mission had failed.

"Maybe Papa Sam will get better enough to take me," Danny had finally said with chin trembling, his head dipping forward to hide the tears that threatened to come.

Henry had nodded. With the help of the root tea, Sam Martin had been slowly but steadily improving—but he had a long way to go before he'd be ready to take his grandson into the wilderness.

"Hey," he'd said to Danny, trying hard to sound cheerful. "There'll be lots of camping trips." He gave him a playful nudge on the shoulder. It hadn't been much consolation. Henry knew it was hard for a boy to wait.

But the rest all had a marvelous time. Three fish were caught and promptly prepared to cook over the open fire. Though the meal was a bit charred—since Mr. Taylor was manning the frying pan and had no experience with open-fire cooking—the boys declared it the best they had ever eaten. They washed their supper down with water from a little spring. Slowly the sun set and the coyotes began to call. Henry noticed a few of the boys crowding in a little closer to the adults in the group, but for the most part they didn't seem to be spooked by the eerie sound.

They had fun trying to point out the different constellations as Henry identified them. "Wow," they said over and over, seeming to be looking at the night heavens for the first time. They'd had no idea that the stars had names.

The adrenaline had been pumping pretty fast, and it took a while to get them all bedded down and quiet. Once they did settle in, it didn't take long for sleep to come.

Henry wasn't sure who was the first one up in the morning. He was an early riser, but the camp was already astir when he opened his eyes. The sun was not even up yet. He crawled from his blankets, rubbing his hands together as he moved to stoke up the morning fire. It was chilly in the foothills, spring or not. None of the boys seemed to have suffered any, he noticed. They were running and pushing and pulling and kicking and tumbling about. If they hadn't been warm overnight, they would certainly soon be warm again now.

He smiled and held a match to the dry grass to start the flames.

"Can we fish again?" asked an eager voice at his elbow.

"Today is the nature hike," Henry responded.

The boy groaned, making it clear he'd rather fish.

"Look," said Henry, "if you want to be a woodsman, you need to know all about the outdoors."

That seemed to satisfy the youngster. He ran off to inform the others that they were going to learn how to be woodsmen. A cheer went up.

Henry did not take them on too long a hike. He knew that even though they were active, they were not used to long treks up and down hills. They spent their time looking and learning—about the grass, the shrubbery, the rock formations, the wildlife. A bull elk even did them the honor of making an appearance. His rack of majestic antlers held high, he tested the air to see if he should be concerned over the presence of the intruders. He did not sound an alarm, just shook his powerful head and marched back into a grove of small poplars and out of sight.

By the time they returned to camp, the boys were weary, and no one argued about resting while the men prepared a noon meal. Henry took his turn at the frying pan. The mouth-watering aroma of frying bacon filled the campsite.

Even as the group rolled up blankets and sorted out belongings, the boys were making plans for their next trip. Henry had to nip in the bud the exuberant plans for another such adventure the following weekend. "Whoa," he stopped them, smiling in spite of himself. "A man has to work for a living, you know."

"When can we do it again?" several voices asked in noisy chorus.

"I'll check the roster and let you know," he promised.

In truth, he would enjoy such an outing almost as much as the boys. *If only Danny would be allowed . . .*

Henry's sadness was not dispelled the next morning at church when all of the boys were excitedly telling of their camping trip—the fish they'd caught and the stars they could name and the food they'd eaten and the hike they'd gone on—a sad-faced Danny listening, close to tears.

Then they were saying they were going camping again. The sergeant had said so. Just as soon as he had some time off.

"Maybe when you grow up you can come too," noted a boy named Tom to Danny. Henry saw the little chin tremble. He wasn't sure if the older boy had intended consolation or meant to be mean. Either way it had the same effect.

Henry clamped his jaw and started down the walk toward home. He'd try again. He had to, for Danny's sake.

He didn't call her first. Just showed up on her porch and rapped on the door. She was wearing an apron over her Sunday dress, a large fork in her hand. He could smell chicken frying.

"I'm sorry to interrupt your Sunday," he began quickly. "I promise not to keep you long."

She nodded. "You'll have to wait while I set the chicken back off the heat."

He nodded agreement and crossed over to his assigned porch chair.

She did not keep him waiting for long, and when she came back she still wore the apron. He rose to his feet, hat in his hands, twisting it round and round in his fingers.

"I'm sure you heard all the talk this morning—among the boys, I mean."

She smiled. "Who could miss it?"

"They had themselves a great time," he admitted.

"I congratulate you."

That wasn't what he had meant. Wasn't what he had wanted to hear.

"That's just boys," he was quick to amend. "They love that kind of outing."

Her silence and closed expression said more than words.

"I was just wondering . . . I mean . . . Danny was pretty disappointed . . . I wondered . . ."

She looked to be immediately on the defensive. He saw her shoulders stiffen. "He's not going off with your boys," she said.

"No . . . not that. I just was wondering if it'd make any difference if I took him . . . alone. So I could watch him full-time. Just the two . . ." He slowed to a stop when he saw her chin begin to tremble. "Look," she managed to say, "I know you can't understand this. I've already lost his father. Do you think I would risk *any* chance of losing him?"

So that was it. She was frightened. Frightened to death of something happening to Danny.

Seeing her there, her face pale, contorted by emotion and painful memories, he wanted to reach for her again. To hold her as he had before. To try to bring comfort. She must still be in deep grief. If only she would let someone ease the sorrow.

He could not move. Could not speak. He swallowed. She had said he couldn't understand. But he did. For years he had shared her pain night after miserable night. He had ached for her. Even shed tears for her. Had prayed that she might find healing.

But he could say none of this now. "I'm sorry," he said instead. "I shouldn't have bothered you. I'm really sorry."

CHAPTER 19

"Where's Laray?"

"We got a call from that rancher about the bear. It's taken some more calves."

"Laray went out to check on it?"

"They're going to take a ride through the back country. See if they can find traces. Maybe where it dens."

"Likely doesn't bother with a den this time of year. Just ranges."

"Well, they're going to see what they can find."

"Did he take his rifle?" Henry wanted to know. A marauding bear could be a formidable foe.

"He took it. The rancher is going to ride with him. In case something happens, there will be someone to cover."

Henry skimmed through the reports

that had come in the post. *Nothing much here that I need to concern myself with,* he thought. *All city stuff.*

He decided to take a ride to check out a complaint from a farmer that someone had snipped one of his fences. He hoped it wasn't true. Maybe a wild animal or some other natural phenomenon broke the wire. But upon close observation, he realized it had indeed been done with wire cutters. He spent some time looking for any clues that might give him a lead, helped the farmer restring the area, and headed back to town to write up his report. They'd have to watch this carefully. Cutting fences was akin to stealing—and there was never a legitimate reason to do so.

Henry had just grabbed a bite at Jessie's when Rogers came through the door. Henry knew without asking that something was wrong. He was on his feet before he'd even set down his coffee cup.

"It's Laray," said Rogers, his face and voice strained.

"He found the bear?"

"It found him. He's mauled—pretty bad."

Henry did not even pause to grab his

Stetson. "Where is he?" he asked as they went for the door.

"The rancher has him in his truck. He'll be coming through here on his way to the hospital. Wanted to know if someone would want to travel along."

"Of course," said Henry. "Meet me at the office."

He nearly ran to the building that housed the detachment, his mind in a whirl. What needed to be done? What could he do? He picked up the phone and dialed the operator. "Get me the hospital," he said crisply. "Emergency."

There was little he could tell the medical people. Only that they would be heading in with a patient who had been mauled by a bear. He had no idea what the injuries were—only that they were said to be serious.

By the time he hung up the phone, Rogers was there. He had retrieved Henry's Stetson.

"I'm going to wait out on Main Street," Henry said. "You keep a lid on things here."

He did not have to wait long until the dust of the rancher's truck signaled the dreaded arrival. The vehicle was traveling far too fast, but Henry was not going to take issue over that.

"He's in the back," called the rancher as soon as he had slowed enough for Henry to leap to the running board. Henry swung himself up and over the stock racks. What he saw made him feel sick.

Laray was bedded on a blanket thrown over straw. His face was so bloodied he was barely recognizable. One arm dangled at a crazy angle, a blood-covered mass protruding from the shreds of a torn jacket and shirt. Henry steeled himself, fighting down the urge to heave.

He knelt in the straw and reached out to the young man's good shoulder. "Laray. It's Delaney. We're going to get you some help."

The truck hit a wash in the road and nearly sent Henry sprawling. He struggled to regain his balance and spoke again. "Just hang on, friend. We'll get you there as soon as we can. Hang on."

The young man's eyelids fluttered ever so lightly—the only response.

Henry felt panic. "Hang on," he said again. "Just hold on. Fight, man. Fight."

"I . . . can't" came the muffled reply. Henry was both relieved and frightened. Relieved that Laray was still conscious.

Frightened because it seemed he had already given up.

"Yes. Yes, you can. You'll make it. Just hang in there."

A small movement of the man's head looked like a refusal.

"Listen," said Henry, grasping him by the uninjured hand. "My father . . . my father was out on patrol, and a madman . . . with a knife . . . jumped him. The guy lashed out at him, catching his leg. He made three big gashes before Dad could subdue him. He managed to tie the fellow to his sled and head his team for home. By then he'd already lost too much blood. He should have died. Never should have made it. But he thought about us—and he wouldn't give up. By the time he staggered into the post, he was almost unconscious.

"We thought we'd lose him even then. But he kept fighting. Kept praying—"

"I can't pray." The man's voice was so low Henry could barely pick up the words. Henry remembered the trip through the storm when the young man had said he let his mother do the praying for him. So at least he knew about prayer, about faith.

"Yes, you can. We can all pray."

"I . . . I turned away."

Henry leaned close to catch the whisper.

"Then turn back. Do you remember the story of the Prodigal Son?"

The head nodded ever so slightly.

"The father was waiting. Waiting for the son to come back. It's not just a nice little story. It's truth. Jesus told the story so those listening would know that they can come back. It only takes a willingness to ask for forgiveness. To confess where we've gone wrong."

Henry feared Laray was slipping into unconsciousness. He dared not do more than stroke the young man's head. He did not know where the injuries were in the mass of blood. He dared not shake him. Who knew what might have happened to his neck? His spine? Henry leaned over close and spoke above the roar of the truck. "Laray, listen to me. If you can't fight, then pray. Pray—so that if you leave this life, you'll be safe in the next. Please, Laray. Pray."

The man on the blood-soaked blanket did not respond. He had slipped into unconsciousness. Henry crossed the unsteady truck box and leaned over to shout into the rancher's window. "Floor it. We've got to get there pronto."

The truck lurched forward, reeling and careening as it hit potholes in the washboard roadbed. Dust was so heavy Henry had to fight for breath. *We'll be lucky if we don't all perish,* he thought, steadying himself while he fought to hold Laray in place.

He breathed a prayer of thanks when they screeched to a stop at the Emergency entrance. Two white-coated attendants were already there with a stretcher. The first one took one look and turned as white as the coat.

"What happened to him?"

"A bear," Henry said, his tone clipped. "Get him in there—quick. There's not much pulse left."

Henry stepped back and watched, hoping and praying they were in time, but fearing it might already be too late. Hanging on to the stretcher, the attendants disappeared through the doors on a run.

The rancher refused to go home until he knew the outcome. Together they waited, both men somber, hushed.

At last the rancher had to talk. "We took saddle horses and started out to where the cattle were grazing. We talked about whether to split up to cover more ground or stick together in case there was trouble. We decided to stick together." The rancher stared with a glazed look at the opposite wall.

"We'd gone two or three miles when I heard a cow bawling. That's how I'd been tipped off before. Cows bawling, looking for a nursing calf. We rode toward the sound, and sure enough, we hadn't gone too far when we spotted this carcass in a wash.

"The Mountie handed me the reins to his horse and decided to take a closer look. There was about a four- or five-foot cutbank at the spot, and we didn't want to take the horses down. He slid over the edge and walked over to the calf. He called up to me. Said it was a fresh kill. Looked around for tracks. Could have been wolves. But it was the bear. He found one clear track in some mud.

"I was watching from up top. He was just turning to come back up when out of the brush this fella came, charging straight for him.

"The horses spooked. By the time I was able to get clear of them and pick up the rifle I'd dropped, that bear was all over him." He stopped and blew out a long breath. "I managed to put it down with one shot. I was scared to death. I knew if I just wounded it, it would be all over for him."

He was shaking so hard he could barely speak.

"Fell right on him. It was all I could do to drag the carcass off enough to get the Mountie freed up. He was a mess. Worst sight I've ever seen in my life."

"You did a great job," Henry tried to assure him.

"We shoulda been prepared for that bear. They're very protective of their kill. I shoulda known better than to let him go down there."

Henry had nothing to offer. It was true. With a fresh kill they should have known the bear wouldn't be far away. He was likely sleeping off his first meal in the shade. But he still would have considered the carcass his possession.

"What say we go find ourselves a cup of coffee? Maybe a sandwich?" asked Henry. The rancher slowly got up to his feet.

"We are most concerned about his arm," the doctor informed them later. Henry was relieved to know Laray was still alive.

"The facial cuts aren't too deep. They'll heal. 'Course he lost a lot of blood—but we hope we have him stabilized. But the arm—it was broken and mangled pretty badly. We're thankful the muscle was still intact. It's going to be a while before we know how much use he'll have. We'll just have to wait and see and pray for the best."

Henry wondered if the doctor had simply used a figure of speech or if he really would be praying.

"You can see him if you like, but we have him heavily sedated."

They decided to see him.

Though he was paler than his hospital pillow and there were tubes and instruments sticking out all over like trees in a forest, Laray looked much better than the last time they had seen him. The blood was all washed away. His scalp and facial cuts were now covered with white gauze.

"Sixty-two stitches in total," the doctor remarked from somewhere behind Henry. "And that was just his head."

Henry winced.

"His arm—we didn't even count."

The arm was swathed in bandages. The bone had been carefully realigned but without a cast. It was strapped to a board to prevent movement, but the lacerations needed time to heal.

"When will he waken?" asked Henry.

"We'll keep him sedated for a while. We'll be giving him transfusions overnight and see what shape he's in by morning. He's going to need quite a bit of help. Lost a good share of his own blood."

Henry was all too aware of that.

"I'd like to be kept informed. If he wakens I'd like to be notified," Henry said.

The doctor nodded. "Just leave your number. I'll have you called."

It was a quiet ride home through the darkness. Henry was exhausted, and he knew the rancher was also. "Thanks for the lift," Henry said as he climbed from the truck. "I'll let you know how it goes."

As tired as he was, Henry stopped to pray for Laray one more time before he climbed into his bed.

———————

"Hello," said Henry the next day, trying to keep his voice even and controlled.

"Hello," murmured Laray from his swath of bandages.

"How's it going?"

Laray tried a smile, but it was crooked because of one of the cuts near his chin. "You tell me," he answered. "I'm not sure what's real and what's a nightmare."

Henry nodded in understanding. "Well . . . you're here. And that's real enough."

"Yeah . . . I guess I'm pretty lucky, eh?"

"You could say that. I like to think it was more than that."

Laray closed his eyes. When he looked back at Henry, they seemed to shine with tears. "Prayer, huh?"

Henry nodded.

"I've been thinking a lot about prayer . . . while I've been lying here."

Henry waited.

"You talked to me about prayer on the way in, didn't you?"

"I did."

"You . . . you said something about the . . . the prodigal . . . coming home."

Henry was surprised that he remembered. That he had even heard. He nodded.

"It made a lot of sense. I've been thinking about it since . . . since I can think again. I decided you were right. That I should come back . . . so I asked for that forgiveness you talked about."

Unable to speak, Henry reached out to squeeze the young man's shoulder.

"I was wondering," Laray went on, "I mean . . . I think my mom would like to hear that. Could you maybe drop her a line? Let her know?"

"I'll do better than that. I'll give her a call. She's waiting for another report anyway."

Laray managed another lopsided smile. "Tell her I'll be fine. Once I'm on my feet again I'll call her myself. Can't move too far yet with all these tubes and this bunged-up arm."

"I'll tell her."

"Just tell her . . . I've come home. She'll be glad to hear that."

"I'm glad to hear it too."

Henry decided he'd better get out of there while he still had control of his emotions. It was enough to know that the young man's wounds would heal. It was even more wonderful to know that the inner person was healing too.

"I'll check back tomorrow," he promised and gave the man a pat on the shoulder.

Henry returned to the street and paused to get his bearings. He needed to find a store that sold Bibles. Laray was going to be needing one, and Henry determined that he'd find one to bring with him on his next visit to see the young man.

Larry's recovery happened far more quickly than they would have dared hope. In two weeks he was released from the hospital, and after a week of recuperating in his simple officer's quarters, he insisted he was bored to death and wanted to get back to work. Henry hesitantly agreed to his returning to the office, even though there was still much repair to be done on his mangled arm.

The small amount of scarring on the young officer's face was nearly miraculous. Two of the cuts to his scalp were a bit deeper, but they would be covered by hair.

"Hey, Buddy," joked Rogers, "you can never go bald or you'll look like a baseball. All those crisscross stitches."

Laray laughed as heartily as any of them.

He insisted he was up to handling a desk job, and they put him to work, more to keep him occupied than anything.

But Henry soon learned how helpful it was to have a man stationed in the office. Laray took the calls, relayed messages, and did a lot of the paper work. He needed only one arm to perform most tasks. This freed the other two men for patrolling and investigating complaints. Henry made sure Laray had plenty of time to do the therapy required for the arm. And every day they breathed a little prayer of thanks that the young man had actually made it back. Henry was reminded again of the power in a mother's prayers.

CHAPTER 20

Christine patted her hair in place and checked the mirror once more. It was not a smiling face that stared back at her. She looked strained. Tense.

There have just been so many things to think about, she argued with herself. *The wedding plans are making me tense and edgy.*

Boyd must have noticed it too. When he had dropped her off at her boardinghouse the evening before, he had accused her of being straight-laced and old-fashioned. *"Too stiff to tie your own shoes"* was the way he had put it. Christine had been hurt by the remark but had tried not to let it show.

He was still pressuring her to move to the Kingsley house. Christine was still stubbornly clinging to the right to follow her conscience. It put a continual strain on the relationship, and Christine felt anxious. In the back of her mind was a niggling fear—one that cautioned her to tread carefully. But always, she quickly smoothed it away. Things would be so much better once they were married.

Boyd had decided they would continue to live with his father. Christine had moments of disappointment, but she knew it made sense.

"No use letting the big house go to waste while we pay rent for some dinky, dingy apartment. Besides—my dad's an easy guy to live with."

It was true. Mr. Kingsley made it easy for Boyd to live with him. He made no demands nor enforced any rules. Christine had no indication that it would be any different with the two of them. Still, she had wished for a place of their own as they settled into marriage.

She had visited with her mother on the phone the evening before. The wedding dress was ready, and there was now only the matter of transporting it to the city.

She dusted a bit of face powder on her nose and patted at her hair again. She felt nervous, and she did not know why. They were just going to Boyd's home to work on the invitations.

She glanced at the clock. He would soon be arriving, and he did not like to be kept waiting. She grabbed a sweater from a chair by the door and hurried from the room.

She was on the sidewalk when he pulled up. He waved her way and leaned across to thrust open the passenger door. "Got your writing hand all warmed up?" he asked with a grin.

Christine returned the smile and slid in beside him.

"Dad's got a list as long as a broom handle," he went on. "I think he knows everyone in town."

"Oh my," laughed Christine. "Sounds like I should have more ink."

"I've a pretty long list of my own," he continued. "How's yours coming?"

"Mine isn't long—not at all. Most of my friends are up North in the Indian villages."

"Well, we sure can't invite them—can we?"

It wasn't so much the words as the way he said them that got Christine's attention. Why *couldn't* they invite them? What did he mean?

"Well," she answered, lifting her chin

slightly, "we could . . . but I wouldn't want to ask them to make that long difficult journey."

She saw his expression darken. But then he seemed to shrug his more somber thoughts aside.

"I just came from the florist," he said, enthusiasm in his voice. "Wanted to be sure he'd have plenty of red roses in. Bloodred, I told him. Big arrangements in white baskets. All across the front. And matching flowers for all the bouquets and the boutonnieres."

Christine felt a twinge of sadness. She had set her heart on an armful of lovely white daisies and blue forget-me-nots.

"We haven't even sent out the invitations yet," she reminded him.

"Meaning?" He sounded annoyed.

Christine shrugged. "Nothing. I just thought that . . . we haven't even talked about flowers . . . or anything. It seems a bit early—"

"If you hope to get what you want, you have to order early."

"Bloodred roses wasn't really what I wanted," she dared to say.

"And what did *you* want?" His tone was not gracious.

"Daisies."

"Daisies? They're cheap."

"They're pretty," she answered.

"They'd cheapen the whole wedding. I'm not standing up front with a bunch of daisies. You might as well use dandelions."

She said no more. It would be red roses. She was sure they would be beautiful. But they would not remind her of open meadows—of singing birds and happy voices. They would not remind her of the North. Her little bit of heritage that she would carry with her into this new life.

"Dad and I have picked out the hotel for the reception. We have an appointment for Saturday to speak . . . What? Why *that* look?" he demanded.

"I thought the bride's parents . . ."

"Normally, yes. But we knew your folks—his being a Mountie and all—would never be able to afford what we want."

Then maybe you should change what you want, Christine wanted to say, but she bit her tongue. She had already pushed him.

"Come here," he said and patted the seat up next to him. "What are you doing so far away?"

Without a word she slid over.

"You know," he said, taking her hand

and squeezing it. "I'm really looking forward to this. Not just the wedding day. Having you. For my wife."

Christine felt her disappointment and frustration melting away. He really was very sweet. She would be so relieved when all the tensions of wedding preparations were over.

She took a deep breath and steeled herself. *Let him make all of the arrangements if it makes him happy. It is, after all, his wedding too.*

She felt lighter as she stepped from the car. She was ready now to begin on the wedding invitations. Even the list "as long as a broom handle."

"You can work at the kitchen table," Boyd said as he ushered her in. "If you have any questions, just holler. Dad and I will be in the den."

So that's how it was to be. Fine. She worked better alone anyway.

Now and then Boyd dropped by on his way to pick up a cold soda or find something to snack on. He always stopped and put an arm around her or toyed with her hair. Once he even placed a kiss on her forehead.

"How's it coming?"

"I have to quit for now. I was just about

to tidy up. I have to get . . ."

He looked angry, but he said nothing.

It was a silent ride back to the boarding-house. When they arrived he pulled her close, but his arms were not gentle.

"After we're married I'll expect to have your company—for the whole evening," he said.

"After we are married—you will," said Christine, touched by his words.

"I'm tired of dropping you off and going it alone. My friends are beginning to see me as a killjoy. I don't fit in with the stags—or the couples. Last night . . ." He dropped the sentence, making Christine stir to look at his face.

"What about last night?"

"Nothing."

He seemed to change his mind. "Yeah—you should know. They all say I'm crazy. Crazy to tie myself to someone who doesn't even know how to have a good time. Someone who thinks a Sunday church service is the outing of the week. They laugh when I tell them that will change."

Christine pulled away. "That won't change. Whatever gave you the idea that it would?"

"Please, Christine," he said, forcing her

head back against his shoulder. "Don't push me."

"No—please—we need to discuss this. It's important."

She used all her strength to move back, giving herself a little space.

"What's to discuss?" His voice was harsh.

"Well, first of all . . . I had no idea . . . you haven't said you were still partying with your friends."

"What did you think I'd do—at nine o'clock at night? Go home and go to bed?" The sneer in his voice felt like a knife in her heart.

"Maybe not go to bed . . . but at least go home," she said, struggling to keep the discussion matter-of-fact.

"To sit and stare at the walls?" He sneered again.

The hurt and betrayal Christine was feeling nearly overcame her. She could barely speak, but she made herself continue.

"And my church—" She choked back tears. "My church will always be important to me. I have no intention of giving it up after I marry. I had hoped . . . have prayed daily . . . that you'd share my faith. No . . . not share mine . . . have one of your own.

That you'd feel . . . understand how—"

"You're not shoving that religion stuff down my throat. I thought I'd made that clear."

The tears were falling freely now. "I've got to go," she whispered and reached for the door.

"I'll see you tomorrow," he called after her. "We need to get those invitations finished."

She did not answer. Did not even turn around.

She cried for most of the night. In the wee hours of the morning she slipped from her bed and turned her anguish into prayer.

She knew what she had to do, but that didn't make it any easier. If she were honest, she would have to admit that she had realized it from the beginning. "Do not be unequally yoked together with unbelievers" rang in her heart. Why did she think she could go directly against what was so clear, what she had known all along, and not pay the consequences? Why did she pretend to be seeking God's direction when she already knew what those directions were? Why had she prayed for His leading, then shut out the voice that would show her the way?

She had been foolish. So foolish. And

now she felt weighed down with pain, with sorrow, with repentance. She could not undo what had been done, but she could prevent any further error. "Lord, please forgive me," she wept. "Help me to do what I must do. . . ."

In the morning her eyes were red and puffy. It would be hard to conceal her night of tears from the world. She splashed cold water over her face and used a bit of makeup. It didn't help much, but it was all she could do. Perhaps folks would think she was coming down with a cold. She certainly hoped so.

She made it through the day. She dragged herself to her room and changed her clothes. Boyd would be coming to pick her up. But she would not be going anywhere this evening. She dared not trust herself to carry through her new resolve with Boyd whispering sweet promises in her ear.

Tears flowing again, she studied the beautiful diamond, then slipped it off her finger and placed it in its black velvet box. She extracted the lovely bracelet from her dresser drawer and set it by the ring. She was glad he had kept most of his gift giving to flowers. At least there weren't that many items to gather up.

When Boyd arrived, she was waiting for him. He pushed open the passenger door, but she did not climb in.

"I need to talk to you," she said from the sidewalk, her voice shaky, serious.

"Climb in. We'll talk."

"No . . . no, I don't want—Would you come out? Please. We'll walk. Over to the park."

"What is this?" He sat where he was.

"Please," she said again. "I did a lot of thinking last night. Praying."

"Oh, that. Look—I'm willing to forget all about that."

"I'm not. I mean . . . I can't."

He swore. "I had no idea it'd shake you all up just because I still go out with the old gang. You expect me to be a monk just—"

"It isn't that."

"Then what. . . ? I get it. It's the religion thing, isn't it?"

She nodded. "It's the religion thing."

He hesitated, then shrugged. "Okay— hang on to your old religion. You'll grow out of it. I don't care."

"I'm not going to grow out of it. Ever. You need to know that."

He slid across the seat until he was at the passenger door. She stood before him, tears now streaming down her face. "I didn't want it like this. To say this here—"

"Then get in." He swore again. "You're making fools of both of us."

"I'm sorry."

"You need to finish up the invitations— not stand out here on the sidewalk—"

"I'll not be finishing the invitations. That's what I'm trying to tell you."

"Then who do you think—?"

"I can't marry you, Boyd." Once the actual words were said, she felt a calmness wash through her being. The tears even stopped, though they still dampened her cheeks.

"What are you talking about?" He truly did not seem to comprehend her words.

"I can't. I'm sorry."

"You have my ring. . . ."

She extended her hand with its black velvet box. "Here's your ring. I'm sorry."

She was totally unprepared for the hand that flashed out and grabbed a handful of her hair, jerking her head so her face was turned upright. "You get that back on your finger right now," he hissed. "You think you can make me the laughingstock of—"

Christine cried out, then bit her lip. With a quick twist she freed herself and scrambled away from his reach. She looked at the bracelet she was holding, threw it into the open door, then whirled to run back to the boardinghouse. She was in a panic that he might follow, but she heard only the screech of the car tires as Boyd sped away.

She cried through another night. This was far more dreadful than she had imagined. She did love him . . . in some strange way. In spite of everything, he was so . . . so courtly, so sweet when he wanted to be. So free with compliments and generous with his gifts. He had made her feel special. Loved. Desired. And she had dared to believe that she was good for him. Would eventually be able to change the dark moods, make up for what his life had lacked, show him the importance of having God in his life, and, with her patient love, draw him to faith.

How had things gone so wrong? There was only one answer. She hadn't listened . . . and obeyed.

———

The next morning she prepared herself for work, bleary-eyed and sober. The emptiness of her ring finger was a constant reminder of the emptiness of her heart. When she entered the office, she saw on her desk the largest bouquet she had ever seen—of flaming roses. Boyd's favorite. The card read, *I love you, Christine. Boyd.*

For a moment she felt remorse for what she had done. He was so tender. Sending his love when she had been the one to break the engagement. So considerate. How could she not but forgive, in return, his angry outburst?

In an instant, though, burning anger filled her being. He did not fight fair. He arrogantly assumed he could have whatever he wanted in life—on his terms.

Fortunately no one else had arrived yet, and she ripped the card from the bouquet, threw it in her wastebasket, and carried the bouquet to the little reception table by the wall. She would not smell them; she would not look at them. She would not claim them.

She sat down at her typewriter and began her work with a vengeance. As the day went on, her emotions subsided, and by the end of the day she was thinking more rationally—but no less determined that it was over.

Christine was in her own room when the usual time came for Boyd to pick her up. Mrs. Green knocked on her door to tell her he was waiting for her outside. To avoid a scene, she went down to meet him. She stiffened when she saw him, but he was so subdued, so gentle in his manner, and so handsome as he stood there that she willed herself to be polite.

"I . . . I came to get you, Christine. We need to talk."

His tone was full of care for her. Full of remorse. But she stepped back a pace and shook her head.

"Please, my love . . . we need to work this out. Whatever . . . your problem, we can sort through it."

Her problem. He was going to help her with her problem. Tears stung her eyes.

"It won't work," she said as firmly as she could over the lump in her throat. "We should have known it wouldn't work. We are . . . too different. Have different values. Different dreams. I'm sorry. So sorry. It will not work."

She saw the anger flash in his eyes again. She stepped back another pace. The black moods of this young man frightened her. She had tried to shut her eyes to the truth, to refuse to acknowledge it . . . but she had always known the deep-seated anger could threaten to explode at any moment.

"Please," she said, lifting a hand, palm out, "don't call again. There is nothing more to say to each other."

She shut the door, flipped the lock, and leaned back against it, tears streaming down her cheeks. She would need to call her parents. What would they think of her? *But I know they love me* was her next thought. She wouldn't be needing that wedding dress. . . .

———————

She was called into Mr. Kingsley's office. She sat in her usual chair, heart pounding.

"This is rather a touchy matter for me," he began after clearing his throat. "A father doesn't like to get involved in . . . in these matters. Boyd tells me you've . . . had a little misunderstanding."

Christine certainly would not have described it that way, but she let it pass.

"Now—whatever this is—I'm sure we can get this worked out. . . ." He paused when he saw Christine was shaking her head.

"We've got those wedding invitations that need to get in the mail. . . ."

Like his son, he wasn't listening.

"Mr. Kingsley, there isn't going to be a wedding," she said quietly but firmly.

"Now, Christine, all brides-to-be get the jitters. It's only natural. You'll feel—"

"No," she said, standing up. "No. This isn't bride's jitters. I was wrong—totally wrong. I should have seen it. We . . . we just . . . it wouldn't have worked."

His brow was furrowing, his eyes narrowing. For a moment he reminded her of his son. "Are you saying you will not even *consider* a reconciliation? That you will not even give my son the benefit of *listening* to his side? He's heartbroken—the boy. Never even went out last night. Heartbroken—and you won't even discuss the matter with him."

"I'm sorry. I can't."

He rose from his own chair. "I'm sorry too," he said, his expression menacing. "I had no idea you were so stubborn. Such a . . . a fool. Boyd would have been able to give you everything. Everything."

No . . . not everything, Christine's heart responded. *Not everything. He was stripping me of my self-respect. My peace of mind. My faith. I would have lived in fear. In subjection . . .*

"Have Miss Stout settle your last pay-
check," the man said briskly.

"You mean. . . ?"

He looked at her. His anger seemed to
have drained away, leaving in its place a
tired, worn-down old man. "It would be
awkward for all of us if you stayed on."

CHAPTER 21

Henry paid little attention to the jangling of the phone. Laray, his left arm still held immobile by a sling, answered it.

"Police. May I help you?" Laray was convinced that if a caller needed an immediate response, it took way too much time to say the full name of the Force.

"Yes. Yes. Yes, ma'am. It's for you, Sergeant," Laray said, covering the mouthpiece.

Henry left his desk and moved toward the wall phone. *What now?*

A distraught woman's voice commanded his full attention. He listened for a few moments, not understanding a thing she was saying.

"Excuse me, ma'am. You're going to have to take a deep breath and start over. I haven't been able to make out—"

He heard a little sob; then she did take a deep breath. "It's Danny. He's . . . he's disappeared."

Danny's mother is on the line flashed through his mind, and every muscle in his body was taut. "What do you mean . . . disappeared?"

"He's . . . gone."

"I'll be right there."

"A child has just been reported lost," he said to the two faces turned his way. "Now, I'm sure he'll turn up at a neighbor's or at some playground. His mother is . . . is very upset. I hope she's jumping to conclusions. I'm going to go check it out." All the same, his own stomach was in a knot of fear.

"It was Sam, wasn't it?" asked Laray, looking stunned.

Henry nodded, already moving toward the door.

"What did she say—?"

"I couldn't get much information. She's rather frantic," he said as he reached for the handle.

"Do you want us to round up a search party?"

"Not yet. Not until I find out a little more. I don't suppose he's gone far."

"If you need that search party—" Rogers was saying as Henry slammed the door and ran to the patrol car.

Henry found her pacing her front porch, her hands clasped together so tightly the knuckles were white. Tears were running down her face as she rushed out to meet him.

"We need to find him," she gasped.

He took her by the shoulders and gently turned her back toward the house. "We'll find him."

"But—" She waved toward the car, indicating her expectation to be whisked away to continue the search.

"First we need to get some information so we'll know where to look."

"If I knew where to look, do you think I'd be standing here?" she blurted out.

He didn't answer but urged her back onto the porch. He motioned to the willow chair, and she understood and sat, wiping away the tears on her cheeks with the palms of her hands. He pulled out his pad and a short stub of a pencil. Not because he needed it, but because it might help her to calm herself enough to think more clearly.

"When did you last see him?"

"This morning . . . when I walked with him to Mrs. Crane's."

"He didn't say anything—about plans—anything like that?"

"No."

"When did you find he was no longer at Mrs. Crane's?"

"She had a doctor's appointment—in the city. I knew that. She arranged with me to leave Danny with my folks when she left."

"So Danny was delivered to your parents?"

"Yes. About eleven o'clock."

"Where was he? In the house? In the yard?"

"I don't know."

"You've talked to your folks?"

She was obviously becoming impatient with his questioning. He knew she wouldn't endure much more.

"Of course I talked to them. My mother called the minute she couldn't find Danny."

"And when was that?"

"When she went out to call him for lunch. He was gone. He wasn't in the yard—or the street. He never does that. Never."

"Had Danny said anything—?"

"Look—we need to find him. Maybe someone's taken him. That spooky man might have come. . . ."

"He's back in prison where he belongs." Henry hadn't intended to give out that information, but he had to alleviate some of her fears. She looked relieved.

"Then what—?"

"He's likely just gone to visit some neighbor kid."

"Danny doesn't do that. He never goes off without asking." She was crying again.

"He might already be back at your folks'."

"No—the neighbor is there. She said she'd call the minute he returned."

"Where are your folks?"

"Out looking."

Henry thought of Mr. Martin with his arthritic knee. He would crawl from house to house if he had to in order to find his grandson.

He stood and tucked away the pad and pencil. "Let's go take a look."

She was only too glad to race toward the car.

He drove the streets slowly, assigning her one side. "Watch for Danny—or any other kids. They might know where he is.

And if you see your mother or father, I'd like to speak with them."

It was on the third street that she pointed to a group of kids in a yard. "There's some. Tony Ambruce is there. He's one of Danny's playmates."

Henry pulled over and got out. "You wait here. I'll be right back."

Approaching the little huddle, he put on his friendliest face. "Hi, fellas. Any of you happen to see Danny around?"

There were several heads that shook in a negative reply. Tony Ambruce's was one of them. Henry was disappointed.

A little girl, sitting on the porch steps with a doll in her arms, spoke up. "I did."

Holding his breath, Henry moved toward her. He certainly didn't want to frighten her into silence.

"You did? Today?"

She nodded her head.

"Where?"

She looked down shyly. He was afraid she was not going to answer. At last, after adjusting the doll's blankets, she looked up. "Over there," she said with a nod of her head. "On the sidewalk."

"What was he doing?"

She shrugged her little shoulders and

looked up again. "Nothin'. Just walkin'."

"Where was he walking?"

"That way." She pointed.

"Did he tell you where he was going?"

"Nope."

"Thanks, sweetie," Henry said, discouraged. The few comments hadn't brought much help.

She looked up again. "I'm Janey."

"Thanks—Janey." He turned to go.

"I know where he was going, though," she said behind him.

He whirled. Was she just delaying the conversation, or did she really have some information?

"Where was he going?"

"Fishin'."

"Fishing?"

She nodded vigorously, fumbling with her dolly's dress button.

"How do you know?"

"'Cause. He had a fishing pole."

"You're sure?"

"Uh-huh. I saw it."

A fishing pole. Henry's thoughts whirled. If it was true—if Danny had decided to go fishing on his own . . . The creek was swollen with spring mountain thaw. Not the place for a five-year-old boy to be on his own.

Soberly he returned to the car. He had to escort Sam back to her folks' house and get that search party down to the creek. But how? And he didn't have a moment to waste.

"I think we'll swing around to your folks' place and see if he might have returned." He hoped his voice didn't give away his concern.

"What did the kids say?"

"Not one of the boys has seen him."

He drove faster than he should have. As he pulled up in front of her parents' house, he prayed they would be back home again. He also prayed that nothing would delay him. Every minute . . .

Her father was on the front porch rubbing his knees. Henry turned to the young woman beside him. "Could you get me a drink, please? I'm awfully parched," he asked her, hoping to have a brief conversation alone with the man.

She looked surprised at the request but went to do as asked.

He spoke quickly the moment the door closed behind her. "I just talked with a little girl who says she saw Danny heading down the sidewalk with a fishing pole." He saw the man's face go pale. There must be something to the story.

Mr. Martin said, "He came in—about eleven-thirty. Said, 'Grandpa, I want to catch a fish.' I didn't pay much attention. Just nodded and said that would be nice. I had no idea he meant *now*."

Sam was coming back through the door again, a glass in hand. Her father was holding his head in his hands.

She looked from the one to the other, automatically handing the water to Henry.

"What. . . ?"

Henry did hope her father would not say anything that would tip her off.

But he did. "Check the back porch," he said to his daughter. "See if my rod is there."

She looked confused but went to check.

"No, it's not there."

"He's gone fishing," he groaned.

"What do you mean?" Her eyes looked wild.

"He took my rod and went fishing."

"Not to the creek?"

He nodded.

Henry stepped forward. "Now don't—" He was going to say worry, but he knew that was senseless. "You stay here with your folks. I'll be in touch as soon as we find him."

"I'm coming."

"There is nothing—"

"I'm his *mother*."

"Please—let us handle it."

"What're you going to do?"

"I'm going to organize a search party—then I'm heading for the creek."

"I'm coming."

Henry knew it was useless to argue. He nodded his head, and she ran toward the waiting car.

It took only a few minutes to relay the information he'd gathered to the men in the office, then he climbed back in the car and spun around in the middle of the street, leaving a small dust storm in his wake.

They didn't speak. There seemed so little to be said.

He drove as far as he dared, then they deserted the car and hiked on foot. He expected her to not keep up, but she would have rushed on ahead had he not scrambled to keep up with her.

They could hear the creek even before they could see it. For the most part, the deep banks still contained it, but the water was swift and churning. Dead tree limbs tumbled and tossed until a bend or a jagged outcropping of rock managed to snag them and hold them fast.

Normally he would have suggested they separate, each take a direction, but he could not do that. What if she spotted the boy— tried a rescue. . . ?

"I think we should try upstream," he said, the first words since they had left town. She didn't answer, just turned in that direction. He could see the anguish in her face.

It was hard walking. Many times the willows along the banks forced them to detour because of their tangled branches. Each time he would come back around as quickly as possible and scan the shoreline— the water's edge, the rocks—for bits of color that didn't belong there. Had he been with anyone else he would have advised them to look for anything that might resemble clothing—in or out of the water. He could not say that to her. She was already close to shock.

Now and then she accepted his help over rough terrain. But she did not complain, even when her hands became scraped from sharp rocks and her clothing was torn on a length of discarded barbed wire.

Once he found a bit of ragged cloth. Hesitantly he held it up, hugely relieved when she shook her head.

Now others began to join them. Soon the creek banks and the surrounding hills were dotted with people—ranchers and farmers, businessmen who had not stopped to change from their pinstripe suits, women, some still wearing their aprons, some carrying babies on a hip, older ones, younger ones, any who could walk and call were out looking for the little boy.

The sun dipped behind a distant mountain. Still they searched. Voices echoing back and forth through the hills calling, "Danny—Danny." It was eerie. It was unreal. Now there were whispered comments and faces filled with fear. The same ones who had prayed to find the little boy now began to fear they might. Surely if he were still wandering the hills or following the swollen waters, they would have already found him.

Darkness began to descend. Henry was aware that little clusters had formed here and there. People were gathering. It soon would be impossible to see.

Rogers came to him. He motioned

Henry apart from Danny's mother and kept his voice low. "They're wondering how much longer. Can't see anymore tonight. We'll need to take it up again in the morning."

Henry hated to agree, but he had to. "Let them go. Have them check in with us in the morning. See if we need help again."

As for him, he couldn't quit yet, wasn't ready to give up. He knew they had already covered every inch up and down the creek for miles.

He didn't say anything when he moved to where Sam was listening to a neighbor woman. He waited for the older woman to move away, then stepped closer. "It's too dark to see tonight. Why don't you ride on home with someone? Try to get some sleep. We'll . . ." What would they do? He really didn't know. He couldn't make any ridiculous promises.

"What are you planning?" she asked, her lips trembling.

He hesitated. He hated to talk about dragging the creek. . . .

He longed for a good dog or two. Maybe he could make a call and have some brought out to the area. But even as he considered this he knew a dog would have a difficult time picking up a scent. The area had been crossed time and again with any number of people.

"I thought I'd just look around for a little while longer—see if the moon comes up."

"I was hoping you'd say that."

He knew she had no intention of going back.

They walked and called and stumbled their way in the darkness. Heavy clouds prevented the moon from lighting the world below.

At last he knew they had to stop. It was getting cold, and neither of them had a jacket.

"We'd better go," he finally said. "We'll start again as soon as the sun comes up."

He could tell she was weeping again. There was no sound, but he saw her brush at her cheeks in the darkness. He wanted to comfort her, but he did not know how. He reached out a hand to take her arm. "Careful, it's rough going here."

She let him lead her back to the car without protest.

It felt good to be in out of the cold. He switched on the motor and started toward town. "Do you want me to take you to your folks?"

"No." That was all . . . just no.

"You might sleep better if—"

"I won't sleep."

He didn't suppose he'd sleep much either.

"You think it's my fault, don't you?" she surprised him by saying.

"Your fault? How?"

"If I'd let him go with the boys. . . . If I had let you—"

"Don't even think like that," he interrupted. "That has nothing to do with this."

"I'm not so sure."

She buried her face in her hands, and sobs shook her frame. He had no idea what to do, so he kept on driving.

"I'm sorry," she finally said, "but I can't face . . ."

He was silent.

"You were right," she went on. "Danny does need to learn things—from a man." She paused to take a deep breath. "Needs a role model. I know that. But I'm just so . . . afraid. When . . . when his father died I decided I never wanted that kind of pain again. Never. It hurt too much. One minute I was alive and happy, and the next . . ." She stared out the window to the blackness beyond. "The police came. A lot of me died that night. I would have died completely if . . . if it wasn't for my faith. Somehow God would get me through it. I hung on to that. And Danny. Danny gave me a reason to live."

He didn't dare reach for her hand. Didn't dare make comment. He had to give her the freedom to open her soul while he just listened.

"I left where I was living. Came here—to a new life. The folks had moved here, and Dad had a good business. But his hands—his arthritis—he couldn't do it anymore. So I took it over. Even let them . . . change my name. It was a joke at first, but soon everybody just accepted it. Including me. I didn't care. I wasn't the person I had been before anyway, so I became Little Sam—or Young Sam—or Lady Sam. Soon it was just Sam." She paused to blow her nose. "That's not my real name."

I know, he wanted to say, but he said nothing.

"I'm sorry," she said suddenly. "I didn't mean—"

"It's good to talk about it," he encouraged her.

She sniffed again. "Yes . . . you'd know about that. You're a policeman."

"I hope I'm more than that," he said softly. "I hope I'm a friend."

She seemed to think about that for a moment. "It does make a difference that we go to the same church. That we both believe." She seemed to gain some confidence from that statement. "Guess that's why I went on so. Not because you're an officer, but because you are a fellow believer."

"It makes a difference," he agreed.

They reached the streets of the town. Lights still burned in the windows of many homes. Families—subdued and concerned for a little boy . . . and his mother.

"You're sure you don't want to stay with your folks?"

"I'm sure. If he comes home . . . he'll come here."

Henry walked her to her front door, wondering what to say, how to say it. He watched her wipe at her cheeks again.

Dear God, he groaned silently, *if someone has to bring her the news that she's lost her son, please don't let it be me.* But immediately he changed his prayer. *If it has to be, help me. Help her. . . .*

"You're sure you'll be all right?"

"As much as I can be under the circumstances."

He nodded.

She moved toward her door. He turned to go, when the light from the streetlamp illuminated something in one of the willow chairs.

He moved cautiously toward the chair and crouched down. The light fell over the face of a very small, very dirty boy, curled up in a ball, a fishing rod tucked in close. He was sound asleep. Henry straightened, his heart pounding, his mind tumbling with prayers of gratitude.

Her back was to him as she fumbled with the lock of the door. He took a step toward her. "Amber."

Her head swung around at the sound of her name.

"Look." She looked, a little cry escaped her throat before she could muffle it with her hand.

"He's fine. Just sleeping." And then she was in his arms, weeping, clinging to his shirtfront, her head buried against his chest as all of the pent-up emotion of the long day poured out in a torrent of tears. He just held her.

CHAPTER 22

She did not cry for long. She was much too anxious to check Danny out for herself. She eased back from Henry and crossed to the child.

"Danny. Danny," she whispered softly, gathering him into her arms.

He stirred and looked at her in confusion. Then he seemed to remember. She picked him up, holding him so tightly he squirmed.

"Where were you?" he asked. "I was worried."

She laughed shakily. Henry wondered if she might become hysterical, but she kept her voice well in control.

"*You* were worried? I was frightened half to death."

He didn't seem to understand her concern. He looked over at Henry. "I went fishing," he said.

"Why? Why did you go off without asking?" she asked her son.

"I did ask," he said simply. "I asked Papa Sam. You said he's my boss when I'm at his house."

"Papa Sam did not know that you meant to go fishing right now. Today."

"He didn't?"

"No . . . he just thought you meant . . . sometime."

He seemed to think about that.

"I couldn't fish anyway," he finally said sadly. "The water was too big."

"Well . . . you're here now . . . safe and sound. Come on. Let's get you to bed."

"Can I have something to eat first?"

"Of course. Come on, I'll get you some cereal and toast."

"Should I take Papa Sam's pole home first?"

"No. Papa Sam's pole can wait for tomorrow. But we do need to call him right away and let him know you're okay."

"Was he worried too?"

"He was. The whole town was. We were all out looking for you," she said with another squeeze.

The news seemed to surprise him.

Henry was waiting to be sure they were going to be okay. He was about to bid her a good-night when she turned back to him.

"You must be starved too. Won't you come in? I don't know what I've got that will cook up in a hurry, but we'll find something."

"How about some cereal?" He grinned.

"That might be it," she answered with a wry smile.

She turned and led the way inside. "You may as well join us in the kitchen," she said as they moved inside. "I need to get this boy fed, cleaned up, and into bed."

She settled Danny into a chair at the table, the first time she let the boy out of her arms.

"Sit up there and I'll get your cereal. Perhaps Sergeant Delaney will pop some bread in the toaster."

They took turns washing their hands at the corner sink, and she wiped off Danny's mud-streaked face and hands. Henry was handed the partial loaf of bread while she poured cereal into a yellow bowl and added the milk. She went to the phone to call her folks.

He thought she might start crying again,

but she was able to maintain her composure. It was not a long conversation. Just a very excited one.

The smell of the toast reminded Henry of just how hungry he was. It had been hours since he'd had anything in his stomach.

While Danny ate, she put on the coffeepot and brought out some bacon and eggs.

Danny had finished about half of the cereal before his eyes began to droop. "I don't think he's going to make it," Henry noted with a chuckle. "He's about to fall asleep in his chow."

She laughed. Such a different sound, he thought. Truly happy. Totally at ease.

"How about if I carry him off?" Henry suggested. "You just lead the way."

The child's head dropped onto Henry's shoulder, and his small arms encircled his neck. Henry fought the urge to kiss his tousled head. He was a tough little guy.

She didn't bother with pajamas, just slipped off his shoes and dusty socks and tucked him in. "I'll finish cleaning him up tomorrow." She stood by the bed, her face showing her wonder at having her son back. She touched his forehead and tucked the blankets around him one more time.

By the time they returned to the kitchen, the coffee was boiling. "Do you mind if I use your phone?" Henry asked. "I've got a couple of officers who will be mighty glad to hear the good news."

While he made his calls, she fried up the bacon and eggs. His stomach rumbled as he hung up the receiver. It was his assignment to make more toast.

They sat down to the simple meal in her neat little blue-and-white kitchen. Henry felt he had never enjoyed a better feast in his entire life.

"I wonder how long he sat in that chair while we combed the creek bank in the dark?" she mused, cup in hand. "Pretty silly, isn't it?"

"Yep," he agreed. "Life can be a little silly at times."

She was quiet for several minutes. He felt her thoughts were far away, and he was not inclined to intrude upon them.

"You called me Amber," she said at last.

He felt his face grow hot.

"How did you know my name?" she wondered.

How could he explain it . . . yet how could he not? He couldn't lie.

She put her coffee cup down and looked

at him evenly, her head propped on one hand. "It was you . . . wasn't it? The Mountie who came?"

He nodded.

"And you knew who I was . . . all this time?"

Another nod.

"You didn't say anything."

"I didn't know what to say."

She smiled, a bit tentatively. "It's ironic. I always told myself that if I ever met that Mountie again, I would give him my thanks."

"Thanks?" He was shocked.

"For being so kind. For trying to help . . . in a terrible situation. For not deserting me."

He could not speak.

"And when I did meet you, all I could do was snap—"

"Well, hardly snap. Although, maybe a little . . . but at least you didn't bite." His teasing lessened the tension of the moment.

She quickly became serious again. "I did appreciate it. Deeply. I still do."

"Thanks," he said simply, but he was stirred inside by this more than he could say.

She picked up her cup again and held it

before her in both hands. "Do you suppose we . . . we could sort of start over?"

"I'd like that." He slid his hand across the table, palm upward. She did not hesitate but reached out to meet his hand. Her fingers curled around his. When she did not immediately let go, he put his other hand over hers.

"You've got a great little boy," he said, meaning it with all his heart.

Her eyes shone with tears, but he knew she was not going to cry again. "I know," she said, her voice a whisper. "And you know what? I think he'd love to go camping."

"I'd like that too." He grinned and she smiled in return.

He released her hand and stood to his feet. "Now I suggest some sleep. Unless I can help with washing up these dishes."

"No dishes. Not tonight. Not for anyone. I'm exhausted."

"Then I'd better get on home. Thanks for the supper. That was the best meal I've ever had."

"You were half starved," she laughed. "You would've eaten cold mashed potatoes."

They both laughed. Then he said,

"Even if I hadn't been so hungry, it still would have been the best meal I've ever had."

"We did have cause to celebrate, didn't we?"

He looked into her face and nodded. He thought she understood.

She followed him to the door. He picked up his hat from the couch and bid her good-night. As she stood there in the wash of soft lamplight, holding the door and trying once again to express her thanks, he wondered just what it would be like to hold her when she wasn't weeping. In his heart he dared hope that it wouldn't be too long until he would know the answer.

———————

A few days later he stopped by the barbershop on the way home. His heart was hammering in his chest. Had he read things wrong? Had she simply been an overwrought mother expressing her relief when she had talked about starting over? What did "starting over" mean to her? Had she really opened the door to friendship— maybe just a crack?

He would soon find out. But the very thought frightened him. Her response to his query would decide about any future relationship.

He fervently hoped there would not be a lineup for her barber chair.

A neighborhood farmer, tucking his billfold in his rear pocket, was just leaving the shop. They nodded a good-morning to one another, and Henry stepped through the door the man held for him.

She was folding the cape, her back to him. He removed his hat, took a deep breath, and said, "Good morning."

She glanced up, catching his image reflected in the mirror, then turned slowly toward him, a smile lighting her lips and her eyes.

"Good morning. Need a haircut already?"

"No ... actually, I was passing by—" Henry began, then quickly amended his statement to, "No, that's not right either. I had to make a detour to get here."

Her smile deepened. She waited for him to go on.

"I was just wondering. I have Saturday off. Thought maybe we could take Danny on that fishing trip. To the lake—not the creek."

He held his breath and waited, heart

thumping so furiously he feared she might hear it.

"He'd love that," she said, and there was not a moment's hesitation.

"And you?"

"I'd like it too."

She sounded as though she really meant it. She hadn't said she'd love it, but her eyes told him she thought she might.

"I'll fix us a lunch," she continued. "What time should we be ready?"

"About ten?"

"Ten sounds great. Danny will be so excited." She gave him another smile that sent a shot of adrenaline to his already overworked heart.

"See you then." He tipped his Stetson and stepped out the door. It was all he could do to keep from shouting. It was going to be awfully hard to wait for Saturday.

———————

They had a wonderful time. Danny was so excited they covered the first three miles of the trip before he could stop chattering. Henry laughed, remembering how it was when he'd been a boy on his way to the lake with a fishing pole. Of course, he'd been considerably older than Danny by the time he'd had his first opportunity, but the happiness was the same.

They spent the morning on the dock. Henry caught a couple of nice-sized jackfish, and Danny managed to land a smaller one. Even his mother tried her hand at fishing. Henry had to show her how to hold the pole. How to watch the bobber. She squealed with delight when a fish struck—but she lost it before she could bring it ashore.

They had their lunch in the shade. It had grown warm, and they felt contented and sleepy. While she repacked the lunch basket, Henry stretched out to look at the softly drifting clouds above them. He grinned as he watched Danny mimic him—on one side, leaning his head on one little fist.

"The clouds are white," mused the little boy.

"They're white," agreed Henry.

"Sometimes they're black."

Henry turned to study the little boy's face. "Do you know what makes the difference?"

"Uh-uh." He shook his head.

"The sun."

"The sun?"

"Yes. If the clouds are too thick to let the sun shine through, we have dark, cloudy days. Sometimes they even look mean and ugly. If the sun can shine on them, they look white and fluffy. Pretty. If we could look at them from the other side, way up where the sun lives, they would always look woolly white and fluffy."

"You mean on God's side?"

"God's side," said Henry. "He has a very different way of seeing things."

Henry was aware that Amber had ceased stacking dishes. Was she, too, thinking about the clouds—the sun—and God?

"I like the white ones best," Danny noted.

"I think we all do. But we need the dark ones. They bring the rain—make things live and grow. But we're always glad when they have done their work and gone away."

Danny sat up and spread out his little-boy hands. " 'Cause if we didn't have rain— we wouldn't have lakes. Then we couldn't go fishin'."

Henry reached out and tousled his hair. "That's right, my little man. And if we're going to catch enough to share with your papa Sam and grandma, we'd best get back at it."

He didn't have to offer a second invitation.

———

They saw one another often. Henry no longer had to wonder if his invitations might be spurned. He was greeted with a smile that touched not just her lips—as she would have welcomed a customer—but lit up her whole face. And Danny always ran to meet him, claiming his hand as he chattered about some new adventure or led him to see an exciting discovery.

One evening the two sat companionably on her front porch after Danny had been tucked in. They listened to the sounds of the evening, drinking cups of steaming coffee. The two willow chairs her father had fashioned—before the arthritis—had been pulled closer together. Within arm's length, Henry noticed. He quietly reached for her hand that rested on the smooth, formed willow arm.

She glanced up, her fingers tightening on his. "It's peaceful . . . isn't it?"

He nodded. He had been feeling the same thing. "Is . . . is life getting . . . a little easier?" His voice was soft.

She nodded. Her grip on his hand tightened.

They sat in silence. He longed to know her thoughts, but he did not want to break into the moment with a question.

At last she spoke again. "For a while I thought that sun above the awfully dark cloud would never shine on me again. But it was there—all the time. On God's side. I just had to let it come through."

He squeezed her fingers. "I'm glad it has."

Nearby crickets chirped a unison song. Somewhere off in the distance a dog barked and was answered by another.

"I . . . I'm going to be making a little trip," said Henry. "I had scheduled some time off to attend my little sister's wedding. Well . . . there isn't to be a wedding now. Things didn't work out." There was some edge to the words. He still ached for Christine and her heartbreak. "I'm still going to go. Up to Athabasca. To my folks'."

"That . . . that will be nice for you."

"I wondered . . . is there any chance you and Danny could come with me?" He turned toward her. The streetlamp illuminated her face, making her hair golden brown, her eyes even more violet.

"I . . . you're sure?"

"I've never been more sure of anything in my life."

"I'd . . . I'd really like that." He thought he saw something glistening at the corner of her eyes.

"The folks will be so happy to meet you. I've told them about you."

"You have?"

"I have. I've . . . I've told them about Amber. Not Sam. Do you mind?"

He thought for a moment that she was going to cry. She didn't. Instead, she lifted her chin and looked at him steadily. "I like that. I would love to be Amber . . . again."

He leaned forward and kissed her gently. It was a promise that she accepted.

CHAPTER 23

It was late when they finally pulled up to the familiar house in Athabasca. The porch light lit the walkway and the log bench on the wooden stoop. Lights from inside splashed out through the curtained windows, making patches of yellow wash over the clipped green lawn. For Henry, it was coming home. But coming home in a different way. Not so much for approval—but for blessing. He knew in his heart that they would love Amber and her small son, but he wanted them to actually share in his joy at finding her again. At being invited by eyes and smile and outstretched hand to share in her life. That was what made Henry's heart sing as he reached down and turned off the ignition, then gave her a smile and a nod.

"Here we are."

Her return smile seemed just a bit hesitant. He took her hand and gave it a little squeeze. "You're going to like them—I just know it."

"That's not what worries me."

Before Henry could respond, the door flew open. A woman stood there, bathed in light from behind. She peered out into the night, hands clasped in front of her, face softly framed by the halo of hair.

"She looks sweet," Amber breathed.

"She is," the young man answered. "She really is."

Amber stirred. "She's waiting."

Henry moved quickly, leaving the car, opening Amber's door, leading her forward.

Elizabeth stood patiently, her face expectant as she watched them come.

"Mama," Henry said as he reached her. He rarely called her Mama. It was his special little term of endearment. He took her in his arms and held her for what seemed a long time. Tears glistened on the older woman's face. He kissed her forehead and she kissed his smooth-shaven cheek before he finally released her.

"This is Amber. My mother."

They exchanged greetings. Amber was given a welcoming embrace. Henry knew they would have much to say to each other.

Other figures crowded into the doorway. Henry was gripped in the bearlike hug of his father, who then greeted the young woman in a more gentle and subdued fashion, yet with great warmth. She smiled her relief to Henry. She was part of the family.

A young woman stepped forward about the same time that a big husky crowded into the circle, his tail wagging his entire body. There was no doubt the dog remembered Henry, and his face got an excited licking when he squatted down to greet his old companion.

But then Henry stood and turned to Christine. He held her close and rocked her back and forth as he signaled his care and concern. She clung to him and wept. Henry was once again sharing another's grief.

"Where's the child?" Elizabeth's question brought everyone's attention back to the present. Henry laughed. "He's sound asleep. In the backseat."

"Oh," murmured Elizabeth in grandmotherly-like care. "Bring the poor little fellow in, and we'll get him to bed."

Henry gave Christine a final kiss on the top of her head and turned to fetch Danny, Amber at his side. They soon returned,

Henry carrying the sleeping boy and Amber his overnight bag.

"Mom—you'll be letting in mosquitoes," Henry joked as Elizabeth stood at the open door.

"I don't think they'll want to come in here," laughed Wynn. "They don't like smoke. Christine cooked supper."

His attempt to lighten the atmosphere worked, and they all laughed together.

"I was just joshing," Wynn eventually explained. "She's a great cook. She even remembers how to make pemmican."

Elizabeth was totally immersed in caring for the young boy. "He's beautiful," she whispered when she finally got a glimpse of the sleeping little face. Henry kissed the boy's head and smoothed back his hair while Elizabeth removed the shoes.

"I've put a cot in the middle room," Elizabeth explained to Amber. "I do hope you don't mind sharing a room with him, dear."

"Not at all."

"I'm afraid it's a bit crowded. Not much room—"

"It will be fine. Just fine."

And it was fine. Clean and fresh and airy with lacy curtains at the windows and a homemade comforter on the two beds. It took little time to get the small boy tucked between snug flannel sheets.

Soon the rest were gathered in the living room. There was no fire in the hearth as the night was warm—not just from the mild weather but from the warmth of this family gathering. They were together once again.

Henry hoped with all his heart—though they had not yet spoken of it—that the family would soon include two new members. As he looked around the room at the happy faces and listened to the soft chatter, he was sure there would be an abundance of welcome. He had never felt happier in his entire life.

———————

The next few days were spent with the Delaneys getting to know Amber and Danny. It was not difficult. Danny was the catalyst that drew them together. They laughed at his antics, shared his adventures, and marveled again at the special gift of childhood. They walked and picnicked, canoed and fished, played games and romped with Teeko. It was relaxing, family-fun time, and it passed all too quickly.

Toward the end of the short visit, when

Henry was confident that Amber felt comfortable left in the company of Elizabeth, he set out to have some private time with his sister. "I think Christine and I will check out that strawberry patch we used to visit."

"That's a good idea," Elizabeth said. "You may not find much left, but there may be a berry or two hiding out." Amber nodded her assent. He had already discussed his plan with her.

The two didn't even reach the old strawberry patch. As soon as they were out of sight of the small town, Christine crossed to a large log and settled herself on it, setting her pail aside. "There aren't any strawberries," she said simply. "We may as well save our energy."

Henry did not argue but lowered himself to the leaf-strewn ground.

"I'd like for us to talk," Henry said directly. They had always been frank and open with each other.

"I wanted to talk too."

He plucked a fresh blade of grass and placed one end in his mouth, enjoying the fresh taste from the broken stem.

"Do you want to tell me about it?"

Christine did, pouring out the entire sorry story of her courtship and breakup.

"I don't need to tell you that you certainly made the right decision," he said when she had finished, wiping away her tears.

"I know," she admitted, "but it sure was not an easy one."

"It'll get easier—as time goes on. You will get over him, you know."

"In a way," said Christine honestly, "I think I already have . . . sort of. I can pray for him now . . . honestly. For his salvation. For his safety. I hear he's joined up. It all frightens me. Dad is sure we'll soon be in a war. He doesn't talk about it much. Doesn't want to worry Mom."

There it was again. That ominous cloud hanging over the country—the entire world. All of the *what if*s and *when*s that kept the world holding its collective breath.

But Christine was continuing. "It's easy for me to understand why Boyd is as he is. But . . . but it's *me* that bothers me."

"You?"

"How could I use such poor judgment? Where were all those lessons in faith? All those things Mom and Dad taught us over the years? I know what the Bible says. How could I have gotten so far off track? I don't know if I'll be able to trust myself again."

He reached out and cuffed the shoe dangling from her foot near his head—the only part of her he could reach without getting up. "Sure you can. It was all still there—buried a bit deep for a while—but still there. You wouldn't let them coerce you into moving in with them. That would have been disastrous. And you did realize—in time—that you couldn't marry the guy. Thank God for that. You could have spent a lifetime being . . . physically abused." Just thinking of it made Henry feel angry, and he threw the stem as far as he could.

"The thing that . . . that bothers me the most is that I *was* praying. All through the relationship . . . I was praying. Asking God to lead me. Asking Him to show me . . . and yet I very nearly made the biggest mistake I could make in life."

"You think God let you down?" asked Henry softly.

"No. No . . . nothing like that. I . . . just tuned Him out. Wouldn't listen to Him speak. It's frightening." She hesitated, and he thought about what she had just said.

"When you really want something," she went on, "you can bend God's will to fit your own. I learned that, and it has really made me think. If you truly want God's will for your life, you need to do a good deal more than pray. You need to listen for the answer . . . and obey, even if it goes against what you had hoped for."

Henry listened and nodded. He was very sorry she had gone through such difficult circumstances. But his kid sister seemed to have learned one of life's most important lessons.

"So where . . . from here?" he asked her.

She laughed. "Well . . . I soon need to get back to gainful employment. The folks have been most tender in nursing my broken heart . . . but one can't go on being babied forever."

"Where will you go?"

"I've looked a bit around here, but there isn't much. I guess I'll go back to the city."

"How about coming back with me?" Henry offered. "Surely there's something you could find in the area . . . and you'd still be with family."

At first she brightened and he thought she was going to agree. Then she shook her head slowly. "I don't think now would be a good time."

"You wouldn't need to hurry. You could live with me and take your time finding—"

"I wasn't thinking of me."

"Then who?"

"You . . . and Amber."

"But that wouldn't—"

"Yes, it would. You've got a wonderful relationship, Henry. One that I pray I will one day enjoy with . . . someone. She's a wonderful girl. I already love her. But she doesn't need me butting in—taking your time and attention. It's enough that there's a child you need to fit into the plan."

At first he was ready to argue, but even as she spoke he realized her wisdom. He was pleased by her unselfishness. Her maturity and insight. He stood to his feet and reached over to give her a playful nudge as they used to do.

"For a kid . . . you're not so dumb. I think you're going to make it."

They grinned affectionately at each other. It was time to pick up the empty berry pail and head for home.

———

The family had only one more day together. The time had gone much too quickly. According to Danny they should just stay where they were. "Why can't we live here?" he asked Elizabeth, looking somber. She gave him a hug and told him his

361

grandparents were anxious for him to get back, but in her heart she knew just how much she would love to keep him close. Well, he had been calling her "Grandma Beth" at her suggestion, and she was sure it was only a matter of time. . . .

"Wouldn't it be wonderful to be a grandparent?" she said to Wynn as they prepared for bed.

He must have known where her thoughts were leading. "He's quite a little guy," he responded with a chuckle.

"She's sweet, too, isn't she?" She knew she did not have to explain.

"She's very sweet."

"I'm so happy for them."

"Aren't you jumping the gun a bit?"

"I don't think so. I see that look in their eyes."

"Like you saw in mine when I was falling for you?" he teased.

"Pawsh. You hid yours so well I never could have guessed," she answered in mock haughtiness.

He pulled her into his arms. "Do you see it now?"

She looked up at him and nodded, her eyes suddenly misty. "I see it now."

"That's what counts," he said and kissed her on the nose.

————

On their last evening, Henry and Amber walked out under the June stars. They had taken few evening strolls because of the ferocity of the mosquitoes, but now with Danny already tucked in for the night, Henry had dared suggest it, and Amber had quickly agreed.

They walked companionably for some time, enjoying the closeness, the peacefulness of the evening. The growing darkness drew a curtain around them into a special nearness of mind and soul.

"When I was a kid, I always listened for the wolves this time of night," Henry said thoughtfully.

"I remember the wolves. I never did learn to like the sound."

"Dad taught me to love them. I almost felt I knew them."

"One of the pack?" she teased.

His hand on hers tightened.

"Now I sort of feel as if I'd like to be the head of a pack of my own."

"Of wolves?" she teased back.

"No . . . not of wolves." They laughed softly together.

He stopped his steps and turned to her, drawing her into his arms. "A people pack," he whispered. "It's been hard to be patient. It seems like years and years of waiting and praying. But now . . . dare I hope?"

Her voice spoke from just below his chin. "I don't know. I'd have to be asked."

"I think I could do that."

He lifted her chin and let the overhead moon light her eyes. "I love you, Amber. You and that wonderful little boy of yours. I would be so proud to have you as my wife. Would you?"

"I'd be happy to join your pack," she answered in a whisper.

Above them the moon seemed to wink at them. The soft wind played wood songs through the poplar trees. Henry sensed it all, yet was aware of nothing—nothing but the song in his heart and the woman in his arms.

She was not weeping.

He wanted to rush back and shout the wonderful news. And he would. Momentarily. He had the feeling no one would be at all surprised. But first he wanted to linger— to savor this special moment of happiness.

She had said yes, and it made his heart sing. Above, beyond the moon and stars, he felt the Father gently smiling down upon them with divine approval from somewhere up above. His heart breathed a sincere prayer of thanksgiving. Truly, God was good.

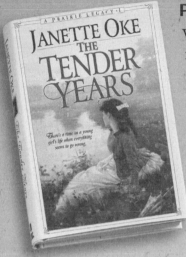